Moonlit Plunge

First I saw the strip of broken balustrade where it had fallen. Then I saw the hair—gleaming, metallic, almost white in the moonlight. I saw the body sprawled there below on the jagged rocks —limp as a doll thrown away by a bored child . . .

Jake said, "She's as dead a dame as I'd care to see. Back's broken; you can tell from the position. Who is it? Mrs. Haven?"

I became conscious of Iris then. She sagged against me, and her voice rose, shrill, jagged.

"She was lying there all the time. Sally was lying there and I didn't know."

Slowly Jake turned to her. His eyes were bright in the moonlight.

"You didn't know it, eh?"

"I didn't," said Iris. "I didn't. I didn't."

The hysteria of that repetition was bad enough. But suddenly I felt as if Sally's terrace was dissolving beneath my feet. Iris was my wife. I had loved her for five years. I knew every in and out of her mind, every inflection of her voice.

She was lying. . . .

PUZZZLE FOR PILGRIMS

by PATRICK QUENTIN

AVON
PUBLISHERS OF BARD, CAMELOT AND DISCUS BOOKS

AVON BOOKS
A division of
The Hearst Corporation
959 Eighth Avenue
New York, New York 10019

Cover photograph by William Douglas King

First Avon Printing, October, 1979

AVON TRADEMARK REG. U.S. PAT. OFF. AND IN
OTHER COUNTRIES, MARCA REGISTRADA, HECHO EN
U.S.A.

Printed in the U.S.A.

PUZZLE for PILGRIMS

CHAPTER ONE

I saw Sally Haven at the bullfight the day before she was killed. I was sitting alone in the Shade Section, wishing I hadn't come, wishing I could get Iris out of my mind. The shock of her leaving me was still crude. I felt exposed, as if anyone could look at me and know at a glance: There's a guy who's lost his wife.

I was sitting there and I saw Sally, that other girl who had become so important. Her bright yellow coat, slung over her shoulders, was like a patch of sunlight. She was walking after a Mexican with seat cushions balanced on his head. Close behind her strolled a young American with cropped red hair and the build of a wrestler. His gaberdine suit was too tight across his shoulders and he wore a dark blue shirt and a red tie. He was the sort of man I imagined she would cultivate if she was in the sex market again, and I guessed she was.

She was paying him no attention, though. She kept looking from side to side through the crowded tiers of *aficionados*. She was only looking for a vacant place, but she was putting too much into it. I knew the type well in Hollywood, rich girls from the Midwest swaggering at Santa Barbara, hoping people would think they were movie stars.

I had never met Sally, but I recognized her at once. There aren't that many blondes in Mexico City. She was smaller than I had expected, too small to have so much spleen in her. But the quick, rather desperate walk was the way I expected it to be. And the hair too. It was beautiful really—shining and very fair, conspicuous here where there was mostly Mexican black hair and Mexican brown skin. But there was too much of it, too great a heaviness, it seemed, for the small head to support.

7

Below, in the circular ring, the *monosabios* in their tight red-and-white coats were scurrying around smoothing the sand. It was almost time for the first bull. One of the few empty places was next to me. I hoped accident wouldn't throw us together. I hoped even more strenuously that she hadn't heard enough about me from Martin and Iris to know who I was. I should have looked on her as an ally. After all, she had lost her husband to my wife. We should have been chummy. But I was fitted too snugly into my unhappiness. I couldn't bear the dreariness of comparing symptoms—particularly not with Sally Haven.

The cushion-seller was coming up the steps toward me. She followed. So did the American. She was about six tiers down when her restless eyes found me. They appraised me as a male body with the blatant appraisal of a woman who has always been too rich to concern herself with modesty. Then the stare changed, a crinkle of speculation coming below her eyes. She smiled and lifted a hand in greeting. She glanced over her shoulder at the man behind her. She didn't seem to say anything, but he stopped following and found a seat near the steps. She came right on toward me after her cushion man, working past the feet of the other people in the row.

"You are Peter Duluth, aren't you? I'm sure I can't be wrong."

Her voice was small and light, rather pretty.

I said, "I recognized you too."

As she stood in front of me, the slung yellow coat giving her shoulders a grotesque military breadth, the whole bullring stretched behind her like a background chosen by a portrait painter. The crowded semicircular tiers of the Sun Section, the orange-yellow sand of the empty ring, the bright strips of advertising—and this tiny girl with the weight of blonde hair, oppressively close in front. Philip de Laszlo might have done it in the 'twenties. Or Zuloaga. Someone expensive and tricky, with a touch of malice too.

"You don't mind if I sit here, do you? After all, it seems absurd for us both to be alone."

It was a complicated situation, of course. But she was making it worse than it had to be. She said that last

8

phrase about our both being alone in an edgy, upslanting voice that ended in a conspiratorial laugh.

"I didn't think you were alone," I said.

"Me? Why, of course I'm alone."

"I thought that big American was with you."

"American?" The wide eyes blinked. "Was there an American? No." She laughed. "You don't imagine I'd be going around with men, do you? Me? Now?"

She stood watching me, waiting for me to invite her to sit down. The pattern of social politeness is one of the hardest patterns in life to break. I'd willingly have seen her in the bullring gored by a bull before I'd have had her seated next to me. But I smiled and said I'd be delighted to have her join me. She gestured to the cushion-vendor. He put a cushion down on the cement seat next to mine. She felt through a small, fancy pocket-book and gave him fifty centavos. He started to complain, asking for a peso. She turned her back and ignored him until he went away.

"They're always trying to gyp you, Mexicans."

I'd heard that about her too, that she was mean with money.

She sat down, tugging at the yellow coat. She was wearing a spray of tuberoses pinned to the lapel. Their odour was so strong that it blotted out the generic bull-ring smell of sweat, dust, and stale beer. Marietta had told me she always wore tuberoses. To me, it's the perfume of coffins.

And just because she was Martin's wife she brought Martin bitterly close. Martin and Iris together—busting my life apart.

Above us, from one of the peanut galleries, trumpets blared over the crowd murmurs. That's how they begin. Doors opened directly in front of us. The old constable on his prancing horse rode across the ring, raised his plumed hat to the judge's box and backed out again, stately and faintly absurd like Don Quixote. High up, the band thumped into a *paso doble* and the garish parade of bull-killers started around the ring.

"You know the name, don't you? Sally Haven." She laughed. "You must have heard it often enough."

"I've heard it."

She laid her small hand on my sleeve and stared up at my face.

"You and me. It's strange, isn't it?"

"It had to happen sooner or later, I guess."

"I don't know whether I'm pleased or not. Just now— I didn't know whether I would wave to you. I didn't know."

The parade circled to whistles and cheers and marched out, leaving the ring empty and somehow ominous. The trumpets sounded again. A man in a brown suit and an American hat pulled back a side door under an advertisement for Carta Blanca beer. The first bull danced hopefully into the sunlight of the ring, black, muscular, and, to me, just like every other bull that passed through those gates.

She watched the animal brightly. "I drove up from Taxco—just to come to the bulls. I don't know why. It was a sudden whim." Her eyes moved again to me. They were a pale, depthless blue. "You have whims, I guess, when you are very unhappy. It's like being pregnant, isn't it?"

"I wouldn't know."

"You're not very unhappy?"

"I've never been pregnant."

I watched the ring vaguely. The peons were confusing the bull with their magenta capes lined with yellow. Already baffled, it charged one cape, got distracted, and charged at another. It looked stupid and rather forlorn, like a cocker spaniel that was being expected to do a trick it couldn't quite remember. One of the peons lost his cape. The bull loomed. The man vaulted over the barrier to safety. The crowd roared and hooted. People above us began to beat a rhythmic tattoo on the cast iron of an advertisement hung beneath their tier. The matador was out now doing his veronicas. My attention slid away.

She said, "You're a theatrical producer in New York, aren't you? I suppose you come for the spectacle."

"I don't know why I come. The bulls bore me."

"They do? How American of you. I suppose you'd rather be at a ball game."

"Maybe I would."

"I love them." She said that with sudden passion. "Oh,

10

I know it's un-chic to admit it. They fascinate me, the bullfights. They're horrible, of course. All that petrified pageantry. Beauty and blood. Blood and the ballet, Peter. It's a marriage feast for death. It's like everything else in this country. Dressed up for death. That's the only thing that excites them, isn't it, death?"

"I don't do much digging around in the Mexican libido."

"But you must feel it."

I was trying to keep her out of my consciousness, but there was a tension, a quivering in her, that made me as aware of her as if her hand had been on my knee.

Her eyes were fixed on the ring. The two picadors had come out on their fantastically upholstered horses. One was aiming his lance at the bull. Obediently, the bull charged. The lance thrust into its back, causing a slow trickle of blood. The bull jabbed at the horse, its horns caught in the upholstery that covered the armour. The horse was thrown back against the barrier. I felt faintly disgusted.

Her hand touched my knee then. It was as persistent as her voice.

"If you don't like it, then why did you come?"

"Because I'm in Mexico, because I'm on my own, because it's Sunday afternoon. Better bulls than bars."

"Ah," she said. "You came because you were alone. Then you haven't found anyone else. They are hurting you as much as they're hurting me."

She was understanding, insidious, probing into my privacy. Soon she'd mention Iris by name. If it happened, I'd do something violent.

As the horse crashed against the barrier, the picador slid clumsily off its back. He dropped his lance and wormed away over the sand. The bull was still jabbing at the horse. The horse fell, its knees folding under it. It lay shivering, its tongue showing, passive to the bull's attack. Sally Haven's hand clutched into my arm, but she wasn't looking at me. The bull had found something to do that it understood. With stubborn concentration, it pounded at the horse. It swerved it around, half exposing its unprotected side. Often the horns split into the horse's stomach then. But this time it didn't happen. One of the

11

peons twitched his cape. The bull lumbered stupidly after him. Sally gave a little sigh. Of disappointment?

The dry heat of her next to me, the odour of the tuberoses, the maimed animal, merged into something horrible in my mind. And I thought that Sally was right. Beneath all the flummery crawled an obsession with death. Death seemed to hang over everything like a black, stifling serape.

The band played a few measures, indicating it was time for the banderilleros. The horse was led hobbling away, while the peons fluttered around the bull. The banderillero came in. He carried two scarlet banderillas, festooned like circus candy. The bull sighted him, lowered its head, and pawed half-heartedly at the sand. The toreros withdrew. Slight in his prissy costume, his plump buttocks emphasized by pink tights, the banderillero stood watching the bull, the two darts pointing at the animal like wizards' wands in a classical ballet. The bull moved toward him. Swiftly the banderillero ran to it, plunged the darts into its neck, and twisted safely away to a roar of applause. He got two more darts and stuck them in. And two more. The virility of the bull and the girlish grace of the banderillero made it more than just a man sticking darts into an animal. It was a sort of sex act, and more blood trickled down the black hide.

The six carnival darts waggled in the bull's back like exotic quills. The band played "La Diana." Half the audience was on its feet, clapping. Sally jumped up too, the two little hands beating each other, her mouth half open, the coat slipping from one shoulder so that the tuberoses were almost in my face.

The ovation over, the matador came in again with his little red cape and sword. I wasn't watching any more. Sally sat down, plucking at the coat. Things were going on in the ring, but they made no sense to me. Just a red rag and a half-dead bull. Everything, the greying of the evening, the screech of the *aficionados*, was ominous now. Even my baffled suffering for Iris seemed something dead. She didn't want me any more. Okay. Why didn't I forget her? Was I like a Mexican bull, in love with the darts in my back?

My attention blinked back to the ring. The matador

12

had the bull stopped. They stood staring at each other for a moment. Then the matador thrust his sword up to its hilt into the animal's back. The bull stood, its head low, gulping. Slowly its knees buckled under it and it sank into bewildered death. The beribboned mules pranced in and dragged the bleeding body away over the sand.

The *aficionados* liked it, but not enthusiastically. I guess it had just been a run-of-the-mill kill.

People stood up and stretched and smoked cigarettes and shouted greetings to each other. Sally sat on, very still. Her face was pale. The skin around her mouth was tight. Something terrifically important and secret seemed to be going on inside her.

She turned to me as if my presence were a sudden discovery. "You don't have a drink with you, do you?"

"I'm sorry."

She laughed, and the laugh was more extreme than it had been before. "Then you haven't taken to drink in your sorrows. In Taxco, they all say I have. They say Sally's lost her husband to a floozy from——"

"Shut up," I said. It had come too quickly. I had no control.

The pale eyes, wide and unblinking, stared. "My dear, do we have to be social—you and I? Just because Iris is your wife, do we have to choose our words daintily? She's acting like a floozy. And if you can't call a floozy a floozy——"

I got up. "I was dumb to let you sit here."

"My dear, why? Can't you face it? Are you hugging a lost love with a hurt behind the eyes?"

"We're people who're not going to like each other. We might as well get this over with as soon as possible. Goodbye."

I started away. She jumped up, after me. Her hand came on my arm, drawing me back. People were watching, grinning. I turned. Her face had quite changed. Her eyes seemed darker and hollow as if something had been opened on to a bottomless void.

"You can't leave me," she said. "Please, please, you can't leave me."

13

It amused me that she, who had behaved as badly as any of the four of us, should decide to be forlorn.

"I imagine I can leave you," I said.

"But I came from Taxco to see you. Can't you understand? They're destroying me between them, Martin and Iris. They're trying to kill me. I've got to have someone. There isn't anyone. Not anyone."

The spray of tuberoses had broken. The heavy blooms were flopped foolishly forward on her lapel.

I patted her arm. "Stay here, little girl, with your bulls."

"But you're on my side." Her small heel was stamping against the cement floor. "You've got to be on my side. They're making you suffer too. I can see it in your face. Don't *go*."

"Sorry," I said. "But I've got a whim to go. You have whims, I guess, when you're very unhappy. It's like being pregnant."

I walked away. When I reached the steps going down to the exit, I could see her yellow coat. She was still standing there, her shoulders hunched. Slowly she moved back to her seat and sat down.

The trumpets sounded high up.

As I left, the second bull was frisking hopefully into the ring.

This time it was a grey one with a white stripe over its eyes. Grey bulls show the blood more.

I was glad Sally had given me an excuse to go.

CHAPTER TWO

I had parked the car a couple of blocks from the bullring. When she left me three weeks before, Iris had bequeathed me her car and her apartmnet. Not that a car and an apartment were much of a substitute for a wife I happened to be in love with.

On the sidewalks, Indians were milling around brightly coloured stalls stocked with pyramids of fruit, pitchers of juices, dough frizzling in skillets over charcoal, and cheap socks. The pavement was cracked and filthy. An old woman followed me, waving a strip of lottery tickets and whining. A small boy whose brown-sugar skin showed through ripped denims claimed to have watched my car. I gave him twenty centavos, backed out past a flower barrow, and started home through the hard mountain sunlight.

Some of the bullfight atmosphere still lingered. None of those bustling people seemed real, just marionettes allowed to wiggle a while before they were shut up in wooden boxes.

I had stopped thinking about Sally Haven. She meant so much to the others. She had become to them the bogy man of the whole set-up. But you have to get adjusted to unhappiness before you look around for someone else to blame. I was still trying to get used to the fact that Iris was gone.

Things had begun to go sour between us in New York. I'd come back from three years in the Pacific war, touchy, restless, and impossible to please. To make it worse, during my absence, Iris had become a famous movie star. I returned to find her with the world at her feet. I had nothing at my feet, just a bunch of ribbons on my chest. I tried to get back into theatrical produc-

15

ing, but things didn't pan out. I had terrific impractical plans for the indefinite future which mostly dissoved into mooning around the house, smoking, drinking. I hated everyone who hadn't gone through what I'd gone through. I hated anyone who was more successful. I guess I almost hated Iris.

She tried, God knows. When she saw our marriage sliding, she threw up her movie career. I should have been grateful, but perversely I felt she was playing the martyr. Her very patience with me seemed an accusation. Because I was insecure I wanted to hurt her, and because she was human she started hurting me back, and I was vulnerable. Our pointless, poignant antagonism climaxed when she moved into the spare bedroom.

The psychiatrist a friend recommended laughed at me and said I was one of hundreds of thousands of ex-Servicemen suffering from a temporary traumatic neurosis. In six months, he said, I would be my pre-war virile self. I told him I had wife trouble. He laughed again and said I was one of millions of ex-Servicemen with wife trouble. The laughter was meant to reassure me, I suppose, and his advice was elementary. I was going through an unattractive phase and taking it out on Iris. It would be better for me and my marriage to sit out the unattractive phase alone.

I told Iris what he'd said and we squabbled about it, the hostility still between us. Finally, in a sort of mental and physical exhaustion, we agreed that she would go away. We were both frightened then, frightened we were destroying something we couldn't afford to destroy.

When she left, she kissed me. It was one of the few physical contacts we'd had recently. She clung to me, and the bitterness went with the feel of her in my arms.

"It'll be all right, won't it, Peter?" she said.

"Yes, it'll be all right."

And I believed it.

She drove to Mexico, partly because it was far away from anything we'd known together, partly because a friend had offered her a house in Taxco.

Maybe the psychiatrist had something. Without Iris, I felt better. All my old tenderness for her returned. I could write to her without self-consciousness. She wrote back—long, cheerful letters at first and then shorter letters, farther apart. I found nothing ominous in that. Iris had never been a letter-writer. I ran into a playscript I liked and embarked upon producing it with high enthusiasm. The show was a smash success. Immediately my self-assurance came back and with it a sharp desire to see Iris. When the show no longer needed me, I wired her lightheartedly and took the next plane to Mexico City. Way up in the air over North America, I thought excitedly of our reunion and kindly of the psychiatrist. When I arrived at Mexico City airport, my dreams made a crash landing.

Because—in the meantime—Iris had met Martin Haven.

She had told me about it that first night in the apartment she had taken in the Calle Londres. She was stricken, but keyed up to it. I had to be told at once, she said. It wasn't a thing we could side-step. I was too stunned to understand then. It all meant nothing except a cold, flat feeling in the stomach and my old sense of inadequacy, creeping over me like ivy creeping over a ruin.

Next morning I met Martin. He came to see me, grotesquely formal as a suitor presenting himself for the approval of his fiancée's family. I realized the full extent of the competition then. Martin was very young and fair and he had charm—charm as irresistible as any I had known. It had to be irresistible to affect me.

It wasn't a charm you could pin down, and there was nothing professional about it. He was English—probably even with some kind of title—and small, light as a boy with a boy's wheat-blond hair and a boy's blue eyes. He was too gentlemanly to broach the delicate situation. He treated me like a rather nice father, talking politeness in his grave English voice and looking at Iris with blind worship.

If I'd followed the manual, I'd have knocked him down and thrown him out of the house. I didn't. Once I rose, formal too, to offer him a cigarette, and I caught a glimpse of our two faces close together in a wall mirror. His was young, golden, and sublimely sure of getting what he wanted; mine was tired, war-gaunt, thirty-fivish. That's really when I lost the battle. Because I thought, "Why shouldn't she prefer this? What in God's name have I got to offer?

After he had left, Iris stood at the window, watching him walk away across the dappled shade and sun of the Calle Londres.

"It's something I couldn't help, Peter."

I wanted to hurt her. "I guess he's more fun than the spare bedroom."

She turned, looking at me. She was thinner, miserably unhappy. "It crept up on me, Peter. I read the novel, the only book he's written. He wrote it after he'd come from England, before he married Sally—when he was living with Marietta."

She watched me whitely, at sea, as if she wanted me to explain something she couldn't understand herself.

"Marietta?" I asked noncommittally.

"His sister."

"His sister."

"Friends lent me the book. Peter, it's wonderful. Perhaps there's genius in it. Then I met them—Martin and Sally."

"In Taxco?"

"In Taxco. Sally has a house. She's stinking rich."

Malice rose. "And you decided she didn't understand him?"

"Peter, please, please, don't make me sound that unattractive. She only married him because people said he was a genius and she couldn't bear not to have the genius belong to her. She has to live on someone else's vitality. He's not a very strong character. He's not been a match for her. He's almost lost."

"He didn't seem lost to me. He looked like a prefect in an English public school with half the rugger team mad for love of him."

The awful thing was that I don't think she was listening to anything I said.

"He was in a trap," she said, almost to herself. "Such a clever trap. Sally's clever. Marietta's the only person he ever really loved, but Sally managed it so that they quarrelled. They don't even speak any more. And he didn't see through her enough to know what was happening. He thought he'd lost his talent, that he never had talent, anyway. He started drinking, behaving impossibly. Sally didn't stop him. Oh, I don't know—I suppose if she couldn't be his inspiration, she preferred it that way, preferred having a wreck of a man so long as he was still tied to her—like a female spider with the shell of the male she's eaten."

"Love's made you very Curiosities-of-Animal-Life-conscious," I said. "Spiders."

"It's made a mess of me." She dropped into a chair, her dark hair dropping forward, hiding her profile. "I don't know anything any more. It's not like any of those Hollywood men. I don't even know if it's love. I don't know what it is. At first I was just sorry for him, and I despised Sally. I talked to him. I told him how good I thought the book was. We made a date to walk in the mountains. Sally didn't catch on. For some reason she didn't think I was dangerous. Martin and I saw each other more and more. . . ."

"Do we need the sordid details?"

She heard that and looked up, not angry, just wilted and suffering. "I've got to make you understand. I was something strong, I suppose. At least he thought I was. And, almost before I knew it, he was relying on me. I felt the whole weight of him. He was clinging to me as something to balance Sally. I was frightened. It was like the Old Man of the Sea." Her shoulders seemed to shrink. "Then, suddenly, it wasn't the Old Man of the Sea any more."

"And he stopped drinking? And he started writing again? And what he started writing was good? All that?"

"Yes." She stared at me defiantly. "Corny, but yes."

"And you alone can make something out of him?"

"Yes."

"And he's very beautiful?"

"If you like—yes."

"And if I said it was all hooey, that you loved me, that this was just—glamour?"

"Peter, don't say it. Please don't say it. It's too late." She jumped up, ran to me, and clutched my arms as if they were the only firm thing in a toppling building. "How can I say it? How can I say that I loved you, that I left New York loving you in spite of all those ghastly times? We were wrong. What we did was horribly wrong. We should have stayed together, stuck it out somehow. I came here, alone, exposed. Without you, there wasn't any armour."

She wasn't crying. Her body was dry and hot in my arms. It was the same body I had known and loved for five years. Part of me wanted to fight for a cause that was obviously lost. Another part remembered Martin's face and my own face in the mirror. Something shrivelled inside me and I knew I wasn't going to fight.

I looked at a bowl of lush pink roses. I wondered if Martin had bought them for her before I came. I could see him with the roses clutched in his hand, sober, rather awkward.

I said quietly, "Okay. What are you going to do?"

Her face was buried against my shoulder, her soft hair brushed my cheek. "He's—he's going to leave Sally. He has friends in Pie de la Cuesta, near Acapulco. He's going there."

"And you?"

Her voice was muffled against the tweed of my jacket. "I'm going to Pie de la Cuesta too."

"In sin?"

"It isn't that way, Peter. He's terribly English about me. He wants to marry me."

"And divorce Sally?"

"She'll raise a howl that they'll hear in Guatemala. But yes. He's going to ask for a divorce."

I was still looking at the roses over her shining head. They wobbled slightly. "And how about me? They say Mexico's a good place for a divorce, short and cheap. Shall I start proceedings to-day?"

She pulled away from me and stared as if that was her death knell instead of her release.

"Peter . . ."

My pride, what there was of it, came out as anger. "For God's sake, what do you expect me to do? Crawl on my hands and knees to you and whine about a broken heart? You've found a man you want more than you want me. Do you imagine it's the first time it's happened since Krafft-Ebing? Do you imagine I'd want to cling to a wife with a head in someone else's gas oven? What's done is done. Take your little genius and mother him and wallow in it."

"Peter . . ."

"And if the wife makes trouble, shoot her over to me." I felt taut and hard, but the way ice is taut and hard over water. "I'll help you get your man if he's too feeble to help himself. God knows, I hope it's heartbreaking when you get him. But if she acts up, I'll fix Sally Haven for you. And I'm not being noble. It's just plain, ornery vindictiveness."

That was too much for her. She stood in front of me, quite still, crying. Large, bright tears wet her lashes and slid down her cheeks.

The futile unhappiness of it all—for me, for her—moved me. I put my arm around her and stroked her hair. I felt then that maybe I was the one with the strength, after all.

"Don't worry, baby," I said softly. "It'll all pan out. And believe it or not, I'll probably live."

Martin left Sally. She let him go with a quietness which should have aroused their suspicions. Iris left too. I helped her pack and drove her to the airport. When she boarded the plane she asked me in a tight voice, not to start divorce proceedings until she gave me the word. We didn't kiss. We shook hands stiffly. I caught a glimpse of her white, obsessed face in the window as the plane roared away.

After that, life had been smooth for them for a few days in Acapulco. That, of course, was just because Sally had been preparing her attack. Then the attack came. I heard about it from Iris. One evening her voice came through thinly on the long-distance wire from the coast.

"Peter, please don't be angry. I've got to talk. There's nobody but you."

Sally had arrived that afternoon and thrown a scene. First she had attacked Iris, calling her every gutter name outside of the dictionary. Then she had turned on Martin. She told Iris that he was wanted by the English police for embezzlement and could never go back there. She said he had consorted with the lowest types in Taxco and that he was a drunk. But those had only been prelimi-naries, getting her tongue in. She came to the point in

21

her own good time. She was never going to give a divorce; she would die before she gave him a divorce. And not only that. For the three years of the marriage, Martin had been penniless; she had given him large sums of money and on each occasion she had made him sign an IOU. If he didn't go back to her, she would sue him for the return of every cent.

"She means it, Peter. It's all lies about Martin. I know. But she can twist things." Iris added forlornly, "Peter, what are we going to do?"

That was what showed me the real extent of my defeat. The thing between us was so dead for her that she was asking my advice as if I were a godfather or an old friend of the family. I wasn't comforting. I growled something about her taking the rough with the smooth and hung up.

Then I went out and got drunk. That's really all Mexico City had to offer me. I couldn't leave, because I had to wait for word from Iris to start divorce proceedings. I had nothing to do. Occasionally, I'd make a half-hearted tourist trip, but Aztec pyramids and Catholic churches aren't much balm. Mostly I hung around bars—not the chromium bars where American businessmen borrow Mexican hats from the orchestra while their wives kick their shoes off under the bars and let their make-up run, but Mexican bars where they play dominoes and shoot dice and sometimes, because it's sissy not to, hit their best friends in the face.

Two weeks before the bullfight I was in a bar, a few days after Iris called, when I met Marietta Haven. In New York it would have been a wild coincidence, my meeting Martin's sister, but in Mexico everyone runs into everyone sooner or later. She was sitting at the bar of La Cucaracha in front of a Martini. We started to talk, not knowing each other. I thought she was the most beautiful girl I had ever seen.

Even now, when I know her as well as the lines on my own palm, I find it difficult to describe Marietta. She was tall and dark as her brother was slight and fair. She was slender, too, like a spray of pussy willow, and there was a quality of spring abut her, fresh, with clean, dark hair and the sort of flawless country skin which made the French pedant write that God, when he created the perfect woman, gave her an English complexion. But that wasn't the essence of Marietta Haven. The real Marietta was always elusive. If she was spring, it was spring with a late frost and a sad backward glance at winter. You felt that, deep inside her, something secret was locked. There's a street in Mexico City called the street of the Ninos Perdidos—the lost children. Sometimes I thought of Marietta like that—a lost child. And sometimes, when her cool green eyes forgot me for her own incalculable reflections, I thought of her as Ixtacihuatl, the Sleeping Woman, the snowbound, brooding volcano that watches over Mexico City.

I never knew why she talked to me that first night, or why, having come into my life, she stayed. But then I never could tell what she was thinking or feeling or even if she was thinking or feeling anything. She hardly ever talked about Martin, Iris, or Sally, either—only an occasional phrase that dropped into the conversation when it was least expected.

We saw each other every day, but there had never been talk of a romance or even of an affair between us. And yet she must have known dozens of other men in Mexico City, although she never spoke of them and I never saw them. Sometimes I wondered if she was a very good person who knew what a raw deal her brother had given me and was trying to make compensation. Sometimes I wondered if she was just a bum after free drinks—because I always paid.

She went everywhere with me, except to the bullfights. She didn't like the bulls. That's why I'd been alone that afternoon when I met Sally.

The drive home from the bullring ended in the quiet, treelined block of the Calle Londres where my apartment was. I left the car on the street and walked to the door leading to my *patio*. Someone had left a large, shiny rooster, with its feet tied together, pegged into the brown strip of grass outside the door. It watched me with a baleful eye.

Near it, but detached from it, an Indian squatted on the sidewalk behind a cloth on which lay a dozen tiny mounds of peanuts and a plate of cucumbers, fancily cut into slices. He was there all day every day. I had never seen him sell anything.

I ducked under the bougainvillæa vine and went up the steps to my apartment, which had its own outside entrance on the second floor. I left myself in, thinking now I was going to dislike the emptiness inside.

But the living-room wasn't empty. Marietta was sitting in a cream brocade chair by the window, drinking tequila. She sat cross-kneed, showing long, thoroughbred legs. She never wore a hat, and her dark hair gleamed in the late sunshine, brown with a touch of gold and seemingly in motion like the gold-splashed water of a trout stream. She was elegant and cool, as always, the way you expected English women to look in the *Tatler* when you hadn't actually seen the *Tatler* for a long time.

She got up and came to me.

"The *velador* let me in, Peter. He's used to me now. He probably thinks I'm the Mexican equivalent of your little piece of fluff."

She had an unopened envelope in her hand. She held it out to me. She wasn't smiling and something was wrong for her. I could tell then at once.

"Here's a letter from your wife," she said. "It's just come special delivery. You'd better read it. I have a feeling something nasty is brewing."

CHAPTER THREE

I opened the thin air-mail envelope.

Peter,—I'm frightened for Martin. Sally was here yesterday. She threatened him again. And this time it's real. She says she knows something. I don't know what it is, but something he's done here, and she says she has proof. She says if he doesn't go back to her, she's going to the police. Why are people like that allowed to live? I hate her. I could kill her. Peter, do you remember that you offered to help me with her? I never dreamed I'd take you up on it. But pride doesn't seem important any more. Martin will never leave me—whatever she does, I know that. Peter, please, someone's got to stop her. I can't. There isn't anyone but you. You might be able to do something. Go to her, talk to her, try and make her see it can't help her to destroy Martin. God, hasn't this made me a monster? Peter, I'm so sorry.

Iris.

I handed the letter to Martin's sister. She was so much a part of my life now that it seemed the natural thing to do.

"I saw Sally at the bullfight," I said. "She came and sat with me."

"Sally at the bullfight. How repulsive." Marietta read the letter and handed it back to me without comment. "I saw her too."

"Where?"

"She came to my house this morning."

"What did she say?"

"A lot of unpleasant things."

"What unpleasant things?"

25

"The sort of unpleasant things she's so good at saying."

"You think it's serious? This threat against Martin?"

Marietta's eyes were green, but so dark a green that sometimes they looked black. She said, "I can't think about Sally on an empty stomach. Let's eat."

We went downstairs, past the rooster and the Indian with his heaped peanuts. I was still sucker enough to feel Iris's unhappiness almost as if it were my own. I thought of Sally with her small head, her heavy hair, her eyes bright with passion while the bull jabbed the horse. She was dangerous, all right. Maybe I should have stayed, tried to do something.

We went to a little Mexican restaurant. Marietta liked Mexican food hot enough to take the plating off the cutlery. English palates seem to go that way in foreign countries. She sat across from me at the rickety table behind a vase of skimpy white daisies, eating the blazing food and looking as cool as her native Thames. In spite of her outer placidity, I could still feel the change in her. She didn't say much, but it wasn't that, because she never said much. It was something more subtle. I wondered if it had to do with Sally's visit to her. Sally hated her, I knew. Marietta had tried to prevent the marriage. There had been a terrific clash.

I could never anticipate Marietta's moods. Because I had no active desire to do anything myself. I found her incalculability refreshing. Sometimes she wanted to go to the most expensive night club in town and dance, gravely and well, all night. Other times she dragged me to the lowest Mexican dives, where she drank tequila straight for hours without the faintest change in her appearance or her behaviour.

That evening, after I had paid the check, she said, "Do you mind if we go to the Delta?"

"It stinks."

"I know it stinks." She gave me that blinding smile of hers which was mocking either me or herself. "We need bad smells. Bad smells and Sally go together."

That was unusual too. That she should mention Sally of her own accord.

As soon as we pushed through the swing doors of the Cantina Delta, the smell came. I had never tried to define it. The ingredients, I felt, were better left unanalysed. A few men lounged at a drab bar to the right. On the left were booths, most of which were filled with boys and men in shirt sleeves, tightly wedged together and jabbering. Unpainted stairs loomed in the centre, leading to a second floor.

Marietta always liked being upstairs. With her proud walk and her black suit, perfectly tailored at the shoulders and the narrow hips, she was preposterously out of place. But hardly an eye was raised to watch her. She was too familiar a sight by now. We went up the stairs. We took one of the tables by the grimy windows that looked down on to the activity of the Calle 16 de Septiembre. That was my doing. With the window tilted open, the smell was less marked.

The waiter brought tequila without our asking. He brought salt and cut limes too. Marietta sprinkled salt on the base of her thumb in the Mexican fashion, sipped the tequila, and nibbled on a slice of lime. She watched me from the clear, unrevealing eyes.

"Worried?" she asked suddenly.

"What about?"

"About Iris."

"You know me by now. That's my theme song."

She put the lime down neatly on the plate with one of her fastidious hands. "Doesn't it ever strike you as idiotic to go on being in love with her?"

"Sure it strikes me as idiotic. So what?"

She looked down through the window at the narrow, cluttered sidewalk below. Her head in profile on the long, white neck reminded me of a tulip. It was absurd, of course. People's heads don't look like tulips.

I said, "Is it serious? This threat Iris talked about?"

Marietta lit one of her own cigarettes. She wouldn't smoke my respectable Belmonts, only the cheapest, strongest Mexican tobacco. She looked up at me over the burning wax match. "Of course."

"Sally has something on Martin?"

She shrugged.

"Something that could get him into trouble with the police?"

"If you like."

27

"What is it?"

Almost angrily, she said, "Do you have to be told everything?"

"Of course not. But she could send Martin to jail?"

"Martin? Me? One of us. Both of us."

"You too?"

She didn't answer. She stubbed her cigarette into the grimy ash tray as neatly as she had put down the squeezed slice of lime.

"But she has proof of this thing?" I insisted.

"Enough. She can twist things. If you've got money, you can twist anything with the police."

"And she'll go through with it?"

"She'll go to the police in Taxco to-morrow if Martin doesn't go back to her. She told me so. I believe her."

"Then Martin goes to jail or goes back to her?"

"I suppose so."

"Then he'll go back to her."

She shook her dark head. "He won't go back. And Sally knows it."

"Why not? Because he loves Iris so much?"

She shook her head again. She was looking beyond me at the Mexican hair, shiny with oil, that showed above the booth behind me.

"No," she said. "Not because he loves Iris."

"Then why?"

Someone at one of the other grimy tables had a guitar. He started to strum softly, flat, monotonous chords.

Marietta was still looking beyond me. She said slowly, "When we were children, we used to live in Hertfordshire." She laughed. "That sounds like Noel Coward, doesn't it?"

"Not particularly."

Unasked, the waiter brought her another tequila.

"The home farm was quite near the house where we lived. There was an apple orchard. We used to go there all the time. Back of it was a steep hill going up to a copse. In spring it was yellow with cowslips—literally yellow."

She drank the tequila. I watched her cool, utterly undamaged face, trying to guess what was in her mind.

"We used to play games, the most elaborate games. Martin always invented them. I never could invent anything. One game was this. We put on old white nightgowns over our clothes. Martin made knobbly staffs out of hawthorn. We started up the hill through the cowslips, leaning on our staffs. Although it wasn't terribly steep, we had to pretend it was. We had to keep on stumbling and falling down and picking up our staffs again and trying to get to the top. But he would never let me get there. I had to die 'tempting it, sprawled there on the cowslips, smelling them. So sweet." She looked at the empty glass. "I was the one who fell by the wayside, Martin said."

"And the point of these juvenile reminiscences?"

She picked up the glass, nursing it. "All the time we were struggling up the hill, we used to sing. Always the same song in horrible, squeaky voices. It was a hymn, really. Perhaps you know it. John Bunyan wrote it, I believe. It was Martin's favourite."

She inverted the glass and put it down again on the table. The man at the other table was still strumming on his guitar.

"It went like this:

> *"He who would valiant be*
> *'Gainst all disaster,*
> *Let him in constancy*
> *Follow the Master.*

> *"There's no discouragement*
> *Shall make him once relent*
> *His first avowed intent*
> *To be a pilgrim."*

She looked at me, her eyes meaningless, almost vacant again. "That's always been Martin's song. And that's always been Martin's way. 'Let him in constancy follow the Master.'"

"The Master being what? His writing?"

"In a way. But mostly Martin—Martin with his cheeks puffed out and his tongue between his teeth driving up to the top of the hill. He knows Sally's wrong for him now. She's stopping him from being a pilgrim. He'll never go back."

"Then he's in for a pilgrimage to jail."

She laughed, a small, secret laugh. "What's jail. It's only a discouragement."

I said, "Marietta, be serious. Should I go to Sally? Try and stop her?"

"If you're that noble, you can talk to her."

"But it won't be any good?"

"It won't do any good."

"Nothing can stop her?"

"Nothing," said Marietta languidly, "except a knife in the back. She has her own hill to climb too. God knows where it leads to, but it's there."

I said, "If you're telling the truth, you'll end up in jail too. You're taking it very calmly, aren't you?"

"Calm, darling?" She laughed the little, secret laugh. "I'm not calm. I'm frightened."

And I realized retroactively that she was telling the truth, that she had been frightened ever since I had found her in my apartment. I knew then that Sally's threat was genuine and that the danger to Martin and to Marietta was real. Marietta didn't frighten easily.

I thought she was a little drunk too. And that was even more unusual.

She was leaning out of the booth and making the Mexican hissing sound to attract the waiter. He nodded, went downstairs and came with another tequila. I didn't try to stop her drinking it. So long as tequila helped her, more power to it.

She raised the glass. "To discouragement."

"Okay, Marietta."

"To you too. You with those sleepy eyes that look so quiet and aren't. You with that square, sailor's face." She watched me sadly. "You're a discouragement, too."

"Me?"

"Because you only like your wife." She tossed back the thick, clean hair. "If only you liked me."

"Marietta, I'm all for you. You know that."

She leaned across the table and put her hand on mine. It wasn't cool.

"You're not all for me. That's the point. I want someone who's all for me." She paused. "Someone was all for me once."

"Who?"

"Martin."

The guitar was still drumming behind her. She twisted around, looking at the man who was playing it.

That was when the American came up the stairs. No one could have missed the American-ness of him. He was tall, husky, with cropped red hair and the swaggering good looks of an Irish cop. He wore a gaberdine suit, a little too tight for his wrestler's body. He also wore a dark blue shirt and a red tie. I recognized him at once as the man who either had or had not been with Sally at the bullfight.

He stared around the bar with faintly amused good humour, making it seem small and foreign. Then he saw us and came straight toward us.

He slapped down a large-knuckled hand on Marietta's shoulder. "Hi, baby. Sorry I'm late. Got tied up with a bottle of rum."

Marietta looked up at him and the blinding smile came. "Hello, Jake." She gestured across the table at me. "Peter, this is Jake." She moved over on the bench. "Sit down, Jake."

He sat down, keeping his hand on her shoulder. She didn't move away.

I said, "I didn't know you had a date, Marietta."

She shrugged vaguely and said again, "This is Jake. He's in the—the—what is it, Jake? No, don't tell me. The citrus business."

"Oranges, lemons, grapefruit, California." Jake grinned at me. "Glad to see you. Lord's the name."

"I've seen you already," I said.

His blue eyes lost their blandness and became guarded, as if I had implied I had seen him somewhere disreputable. "You have?"

"At the bullfight this afternoon."

The grin came again. "Why, sure."

"I thought you were with a friend of mine. That's how I noticed you."

"With a friend of yours? No, sir, not me. Only hit this town two days ago. Haven't met a soul except Marietta." He squeezed her shoulder. "We met up yesterday and did the town, didn't we, baby?"

"I suppose so." Marietta had become very English and precise. "Yes, I suppose that's what you'd call it."

Jake showed me his strong white teeth again. "She dated me up for ten to-night here." He looked around. "It's a dump, isn't it? I guess Marietta goes for dumps."

I shouldn't have been surpised at Marietta's citrus-grower. Certainly I shouldn't have been jealous. I had no claims on her. I had made that clear by my stubborn love for Iris. But as Jake went on talking "man's talk" to me while his hand pawed Marietta's shoulder, I felt an unreasonable jealousy and disgust. Perhaps I was disgusted by Marietta, who was too beautiful and had too much integrity to be mauled by a great hunk of male flesh in a cheap bar. Perhaps I was disgusted by the man for not realizing that Marietta was so much, much more than the tramp he seemed to take her for.

I didn't like him, anyway. For some reason I didn't believe in his fruit farm. There was something subtly but distinctly citified about him. A mechanic, maybe, who'd worked his way up to a garage of his own. And I didn't believe in his amiability, in spite of the friendly grin. It was laid on too thick, and his blue, Irish eyes were too alert.

Suddenly, because I didn't trust him, I started wondering whether both he and Sally were lying. Perhaps they had been at the bullfight together and Sally had given him the high sign to leave her when she noticed me. I knew how devious Sally could be and, since she was essentially sinister, I wondered whether this man could be sinister too.

Having introduced him, Marietta seemed to have lost interest in him. She had drifted into one of her remote, impregnable silences. I wondered whether she even knew what his hand was doing.

An Indian with a big sun-bleached straw hat and a beribboned guitar had come to the table and was standing, staring at us patiently. He wasn't the man who had been playing. He was a professional, an itinerant musician from the street.

Jake noticed him. He prodded Marietta.

"Hey, baby, what's the name of your song? What's the song you had them playing all last night? 'La Borrachitá'? Yeah, that's it."

He turned to the musician and spoke to him in surprisingly native-sounding Spanish. His face unchanged, the Indian strummed the guitar and started to sing in a high, harsh voice that was oddly moving. I knew the song, of course. It's been knocking around Mexico for years. It's pretty and sad. It had been a favourite of Iris's in the States. Someone had sent her a record.

As I listened I thought of Iris, and self-pity crept over me. Everything seemed sad, unnecessarily sad, sadness invented for me only.

The flat voice, empty of all inflection, went on:

> *"Borrachitá, me voy par olvidarle.*
> *Le quero mucho y el también me quere,*
> *Borrachitá, me voy hasta la capital*
> *Par servirme al patron*
> *Que me mandó llamar ante ayer."*

A plaintive chord twanged into silence. Jake grinned, said "Swell," and gave the Indian a peso. The Indian went away.

I'd been too tied to my own nostalgia to look at Marietta. But I did look then. She was sitting staring straight ahead of her, her chin cupped in her hand. Tears were rolling slowly down her cheeks.

She picked up her pocketbook, rose, and said very gravely, "I'm going home now."

Jake jumped up, fussing around her, keeping his hand on her elbow. "Baby, what's the trouble? Got the blues?"

"I'm going home now."

"Sure, sure, baby. Don't worry. Jake'll take you home, tuck you up for bye-bye."

He was guiding her away from the table. Marietta stopped and turned to look back at me. Tears still glistened in her eyes.

"Peter . . ."

Her hand went out to me and then dropped down. I knew she was trying to ask me not to let her go home with Jake. But I was confused and mad and somehow hurt that she'd sneaked the date up on me. I wanted to hurt her too.

I said, "I guess your friend can take care of you okay. Night, Jake. See you, Marietta."

She turned to Jake without a word. Submissively she let him lead her toward the stairs.

As they passed a crowded table, two of the Mexicans at it started screaming. They leaped up, tossing back their long black hair, cursing and hitting wildly at each other. One of them staggered back against the wall and whipped out a knife.

Jake swung round, and spat Spanish at them. From nowhere, it seemed, there was a gun in his hand. He covered them both, leaned forward grinning, and flicked the knife out of the Mexican's hand. Both men slumped sulkily into their seats. Marietta was staring blankly. Jake slipped the gun back into his coat, waved back at me, and took her arm again.

I saw their heads as they descended the stairs, Marietta's wonderful dark head and Jake's cropped red hair. Then they were gone.

Alone at the table, a sense of frustration swept over me. Marietta had gone off with a gun-toting citrus-grower she didn't want, who might also be a hidden ally of Sally's. I was sitting in a bar, and nothing had been done. Martin wouldn't go back to Sally. Sally would go to the police. Martin, and maybe Marietta, would have to face some criminal charge which was neither true nor effectively cooked up.

I should have been happy about it. If things worked out that way, Iris might come back to me. But what would be the good of that? Who wanted a wife when she was eating her heart out for another man?

Suddenly I decided I'd spar with Sally and fight it out for Iris and Marietta and Martin. God knows, it was against my own interests, "noble" dime-store chivalry. But anything was better than this—anything.

I thought of Martin then, beautiful, golden Martin in the field of yellow cowslips—always getting to the top of the hill and never letting Marietta get there. I thought of Iris too, in Acapulco, tormenting herself with fear of what Sally could do to Martin.

Martin with his public-school prefect's gravity, his charm, his so-called genius, and his dubious career, Martin whom three women wanted and who wanted only to be a pilgrim.

They all called Sally a monster. But Sally was only fighting to keep her husband, the way I was not fighting to keep my wife.

It seemed to me then that the real monster was Martin.

I guess I was a little drunk.

CHAPTER FOUR

I drove home past the Alameda, dark and faintly sinister now, and down the stately boulevard of the Paseo de la Reforma. Mexico City shuts up early at night. Except for the occasional glitter of a night club entrance, the town stretched around me emptily, not like a real town, like something two-dimensional built out of cardboard on a Hollywood set.

At the Calle Londres, the Indian and his peanuts had gone. So had the rooster. But a car, a new scarlet convertible coupé, was parked outside my house. I drove past to the garage, left my car, and walked back. When I reached the iron gate to the *patio* and ran for the *velador*, the red coupé was still there. I didn't bother with it until I heard its door open behind me and the patter of high heels on the cement sidewalk.

I turned. Sally Haven was there, the yellow coat still slung over her shoulders. The nearest street light was some way off. It made the yellow coat gleam, and the heavy yellow hair, and her eyes. The rest of her was in shadow. The curious chiaroscuro exaggerated her dollish smallness.

"I waited. I had to see you. It was cold, but I waited."

Her hand moved forward and touched mine. It was light as an insect against my skin with the dry hardness of an insect.

The chain clattered off and the *velador* was opening the gate.

"Come in," I said, hating the thought of it, but remembering my decision.

She snuggled deeper into the coat and slid her hand through my arm.

"It was cold, but I waited. I didn't want to miss you."

36

I took her up the iron staircase and let her into the apartment. I turned on the lights. The apartment was a suite in one of those majestic French-style mansions that had been built in Porfirio Díaz's day. The original Second Empire furniture was still there.

"Charming," said Sally. And then, "Iris found it, didn't she?" She let the coat drop off her shoulders on to the floor and left it there, not bothering. Her eyes, never missing anything, rested on the two empty glasses and the ash tray with Marietta's lipstick-stained butts. "A visitor," she said. "A woman." She laughed, half coquettishly. "And at the bullfight I was so sorry for you because you said you were alone."

She dropped on to the couch without being asked, tucking her legs under her. She had the imperial rudeness of the well-heeled Midwestern girl who assumes that it's a privilege for any man to have such a combination of femininity and fortune in his house. I tried to remember where she came from. Pittsburgh? Chicago! And the money? Ham? Soft drinks?

"Tequila?" I said. "I'm afraid it's all I have."

She nodded. She took a long jade cigarette-holder from her pocketbook, fitted a cigarette into it, and lit it. The cigarette-holder was preposterous. But you couldn't laugh at her. Her eyes were too alive and there was a controlled excitement in her that changed the atmosphere of the room, somehow made it dangerous.

I pushed a glass across to her and sat down on a chair near her, holding my own glass.

She lifted the glass to me and said, *"Salud."*

"Salud," I said, "Why have you come? Things didn't go too well between us at the bullfight."

"I know." She smiled a bright smile with nothing in it except that incalculable excitement. "I know. It was my fault. I'm sorry. I shouldn't have said that about Iris."

"You shouldn't."

"I shouldn't have said it because it was against my own interests." She leaned forward sharply. "You're still in love with her, aren't you?"

"Do we have to go into who loves who?"

"You love her. You want her back. I love Martin."

"You do?"

37

"Oh, you don't believe that. You've been listening to them. The filthy things they say. Can't you see through them? Can't you see they're only trying to make me the villain to justify themselves? I love Martin. He's the only man I ever loved."

Her eyes were trying to be little-girl eyes, wide and hurt. There was a plangency too in her voice.

"I was so good to him. I believed in his talent. I gave him everything. When I met him he was nothing, living in a filthy little room with Marietta, penniless, bumming drinks at Paco's from the tourists, consorting with the Mexicans, the boys who work in the silver mines, the lowest type of Mexicans."

She turned her head. "They left England when the war started because Martin was afraid of being drafted into the Army. I think there were other reasons too. The family disowned them. It's a good family. But they disowned them. They had no money, nothing. He wrote the book, but he didn't make anything on it, not a cent. I wanted to save him from the awful, squalid life he'd dropped into. I wanted him to have everything he should have. And he took everything. Everything I offered he took. Why I've given him thousands and thousands of dollars in cash. And I can prove it. I made him sign IOU's. I did that for his own good, to give him some conception of decency about money. I have the IOU's. I can prove it."

She turned with a sharp movement to pick up her pocketbook. I thought she was going to search through it and produce the IOU's to prove it.

I said, "Okay. I believe you. You gave him thousands of dollars. You love him."

"I love him." She shook the heavy gold hair passionately. "I love him. And I'm never going to divorce him—never."

"And what if he doesn't love you?"

"Love me?" She laughed. "Of course he doesn't love me. He hates me. He hates me because he knows he owes everything to me. He knows I called his bluff. I gave him everything a writer could want, he couldn't write. I gave him everything a man could want, and he flunked that too. I made him see himself for what he is, a sham, an emptiness—a nothing."

"Such language about the man you love."

"Why shouldn't I say it? It's true. And it doesn't make any difference. He's mine. He belongs to me. I'm going to get him back."

I lit a cigarette, my head aching faintly. "Okay. You're going to get him back. But why bother to tell me about it?"

"Because I want you to know. You see, I have a plan. It'll work. I'll get Martin back. Then you'll have Iris again."

"Thank you."

"You do want her, don't you?" She leaned toward me again over the coffee table, her eyes hungry. "Maybe you don't. Maybe you feel the way I feel, that a woman like that doesn't deserve to——"

"Let's not talk about Iris. You've got a plan. Tell me your plan."

I knew pretty much what it was, of course. I had no plan myself, just to let her talk and see which way the wind lay. I didn't like anything about it. Not so much what she was saying, but the aura around her. They had always said she was dangerous, and the danger was as evident as a perfume or a scarf knotted at her tiny neck. I couldn't analyse it. I just knew that her reactions were unstable, not like reactions I knew. She was unpredictable—and desperate.

"It's something they did," she said. She wore a heavy silver bracelet on her left wrist. As she moved, it clattered. "He and Marietta. Marietta's his sister. You know that?"

I nodded.

"Marietta's worse than he is. She's bad, really bad. And they were so nastily close. She was his evil genius, really." Her lips curled in a smile of remembered satisfaction. "At least I managed to break that up."

"And how did you do it?" I asked casually. I didn't want her to think I was interested in Marietta one way or the other.

"By telling him the truth about her."

"And the truth about Marietta?"

Her tiny hand plucked the cigarette stub out of the holder and tossed it into an ash tray. "That she's a bum." She giggled. It sounded like water dribbling from a leaky faucet. "He wouldn't believe it at first, not until I showed him some of the men she'd made fools out of, made him see it had to be true. And he hates her now. It's all vanity. He thought he was the only man for her. He couldn't abide thinking of his sister playing hooky from worshipping at his shrine. He couldn't bear to think that all the time she'd been even worse than him—just a tramp."

I thought of Marietta's cool, snowbound beauty. I thought of Marietta never getting to the top of the cow-slip hill. I thought of the citrus-grower from Southern California with the big, self-confident hands and the gun.

"It's something they did," she said again. Her left hand, with the ponderous bracelet sagging at the bird wrist, was clutching her tucked-in legs so that she was in a small, tight ball on the couch. "Something with a tourist in Taxco. Before our marriage. The police thought it was a guide. They were never sure. But I know. I can break it to the police. I can get them both jailed. I have proof."

She was always talking about having proof. I had a vision of her ceaselessly patterning around, the doll nose poking out from under the canopy of hair, peering in closets, scurrying through desks, finding proof against other people. I wondered vaguely, if she was telling the truth, if Martin was really a shoddy crook. Not that it mattered. Iris would have stuck to him if he murdered his mother.

"And I told him," she was saying. "I told her too— Marietta. I went to them both and I told them what I know. I told them I'd go to the police tomorrow if Martin didn't come back." She turned from profile to face me with a smile that was sure of itself and sure of my de-lighted approval. "That's my plan. That's what I want you to know. I'm going to the police to-morrow if Martin doesn't come back."

It was then that I began to despise this little disturbed girl. I despised her for the pleasure she took in her own infantile craftiness and for the stupidity of her malice. She said she loved her husband. She didn't, of course. I knew Iris was right now. He was just another thing she had bought, and the losing of it galled her vanity. She said she wanted him back and yet, to get him back, she was prepared to do something that would cement his hatred of her into a permanent mould. She made no sense. Nothing made sense about her except a desire to destroy, blind as an owl's eyes in the sunlight. But because I despised her, I didn't minimize the potential danger in her. Martin wouldn't go back. She would go to the police. All hell would break loose—unless I could do something.

I crossed to the couch and sat down beside her. With the white throat and the small head, tilted backwards by the mass of hair, she had a strange sensuality which didn't excite me, but which made me aware of its existence.

I said, "You think Martin will come back to-morrow?"

"If he's scared enough."

"And that'll satisfy you, having him back on those terms?"

"Yes," she said and to me there was something almost obscene in the monosyllable.

"And if he's not scared enough?"

She laughed. "Oh, he may try to kill me. So may Marietta." She leaned toward me, her thin fingers gripping my wrist. The laughter was out of her eyes now, and there was something else there that was almost excitement. "I mean that, you know. It's true. What I've done, it's dangerous. Because they're utterly unscrupulous, both of them. I can send them to jail. They know that. And I haven't changed my will yet. I've left everything to Martin. They know that too. Oh, yes, they may try to kill me. So may Iris. She's so hot for him, so eaten up with him. If she knew she couldn't get him any other way . . ."

To me, that seemed the very apogee of fake.

In my distaste, I forgot to handle her.

I said, "Have you ever been kicked very hard in the pants?"

Her wide eyes blinked up at me. "Kicked? Me?"

"Don't you see what you're doing. Haven't you the faintest idea about yourself?"

"Have I?" Her eyes were still excited. Something

about their expression brought back memories of her jumping up from her seat at the bullfight, clapping her little hands, staring at the gay, festooned banderillas flapping like deplumed feathers out of the bull's bleeding back. "Have I? Tell me, Peter, tell me about me."

"It's quite elementary."

"Is it? Is it? What am I?" Her face was almost touching my shoulder. "What am I?"

"Principally," I said, "you're a bitch. A classic example of a rich bitch. You bought a poor man who didn't want you, because you smelled a bargain genius. You lost him. And once you'd lost him, you became nothing —just another piece of unwanted woman. You can't bear being off the centre of the stage. You had to get back. And because you hadn't any legitimate reason to get back, you had to do it by mean little ruses, threats, scenes, wielding feeble little whips, trying to destroy people's happiness, fiddling with danger like a child playing with firecrackers. You don't want Martin. You just want attention. And a lousy job you're making of it. In the last half-hour, you've been the heartbroken wife, the avenging fury, and now—the potential murderee. That's too many roles. You want me to think you're interesting. I don't. I think you're a goddamn bore. If I were you, know what I'd do?"

She didn't seem to be mad. She had moved even closer, uncurling her little legs. Her golden hair was brushing the lapel of my coat.

"No, Peter. No. What would you do if you were I?"

"I'd go back to Chicago or Pittsburgh or wherever it is and sit on my pile of dollars until another man comes along who's stupid enough to think the money's worth the gamble. Marry him. After that, do anything you want with him. I won't be interested because by then you'll be out of my life."

She had half closed her eyes. She had surprisingly heavy lids, like a doll's. She sank toward me. Her arms slid up me; her hands, with the thick bracelet on the thin wrist, twined around my neck.

"You think that, Peter? You really think that?"

I put my hands on her small waist to push her away. Suddenly her lips dug into mine.

"You understand me," she breathed. "I thought you would. When I first saw you at the bullfight, I thought you'd understand me. Such shoulders. A fighter's jaw. A man's face."

"For God's sake." I was angry because she'd fooled me. I'd never expected this.

Her lips slide to mine again. She was slumped against me. She was surprisingly heavy for her smallness, like the eyelids. She was crooning words of endearment. She wanted me. She needed a real man like me, someone who was strong, who could slap her down. She'd always known weak men, men like Martin sapping her strength, making her the strong one. She didn't want to be strong. She didn't want to boss. She wanted to be bossed, she wanted to be kicked. Her body against mine was warm, but it wasn't real warmth, it was the warmth of a fever. It was repulsive to me, just as the soft, monotonous coo of her voice was repulsive.

I pushed her away. I held her there, my hands on her arms. She stared back at me glassily, her lips half parted.

"You don't want me," she said.

"No," I said.

"Why?" Her eyes flashed with weak venom. "It's Iris."

"I didn't say so."

"You've got someone else?" Her little hands flashed down, gripping my wrists. "There's someone else. The woman with the glass, the woman with the cigarette butts."

I said, "It's none of your business whether there is or not."

"Who is she?" Her nails were digging into the skin of my wrists. I flicked her hands off. "Who is she? Tell me."

"You'd better go home," I said. "Throw Martin and Marietta in jail. Foul up everything. Go on. You're not worth bothering about."

"Tell me who she is." Tears were staining her cheeks, hot tears of fury. "Why should everyone get something but me? Why am I always left out? Why should you have someone else?" She stamped her foot against the carpet. "Tell me who she is."

She'd had a stray sex impulse. She hadn't been able to satisfy it. It was like having a lunatic on my hands.

Maybe it wasn't like. Maybe it was actually having a lunatic on my hands.

I got up. I slung an arm around her and dragged her up too. I went for the yellow coat, picked it off the floor, and threw it around her shaking shoulders.

"You'd better go home."

She stood there, her hands clenched at her sides.

"Who's the woman? I've got to know. Who's the woman?"

The door opened then. I heard the *velador* muttering, *"Gracias, Señorita."* I turned around.

Marietta had come into the room.

CHAPTER FIVE

She came toward us, tall, impeccable. The dark, clean hair hung loose around her shoulders. Seeing her over Sally's disordered face was like a draught of spring water after a mouthful of dust. She had never looked lovelier, but I wished she hadn't chosen this of all moments to come.

She glanced at Sally, making no situation out of it at all.

"Hello, Sally. Hello, Peter."

I don't think Sally had realized that anyone had come in until she heard Marietta's voice. She spun around, the gold hair swinging like a bell. She backed up against me, her thin, hot body pressing. I couldn't see her face, but I could imagine it.

"You!" she said.

Marietta smiled her blank smile. "I never know how to reply when people say 'You.' "

"I might have guessed." Sally whirled around. Her grabbing little hands caught my sleeves. She glared up at me, her eyes still hectic. "It's Marietta. The glass, the cigarette butts. It's Marietta. You're just another of Marietta's——"

"Quiet," I said.

Her fingers dug into my coat. She was trying to hurt me. She couldn't.

"You're on their side. You're just a goddamn complacent husband. Why didn't I guess it? Marietta got you the way she's got every other man in Mexico. And you've been laughing at me. All the time, you've been on their side, laughing at me."

Marietta was watching her, more curious than anything else.

45

I said, "I still think you'd better go home, Sally."

She wasn't listening. She was abandoned to fury as if to a lover.

"You'll be sorry." She lunged away from me, staring at Marietta, including her in her malice. "All of you. You'll be sorry. To-morrow, I'll make you pay. If it's the last thing I do. I'll make you pay."

She swept her hand over her forehead. The gesture was as corny as Matilda, the Beautiful Shopgirl. But it didn't make her any less authentic and horrible. She started for the door, her high heels tap-tapping. She reached it. She tugged it open. Then she turned to Marietta, the yellow coat swaying capelike around her shoulders. Bare malignancy was in her eyes.

"To-morrow," she said, "you'll be in jail."

And she laughed.

I could hear the laughter fading as she clattered down the iron stairway to the *patio*.

Marietta dropped on to the sofa. Now Sally was gone, the springiness had left her. She looked tired and white.

"Nice girl, Sally," I said.

"Such original phrases. *I'll make you pay if it's the last thing I do.* She should copyright it." Marietta glanced up, shaking the dark hair back. "Got any tequila left, Peter?"

I poured her some. My hand was unsteady. Sally had done that to me. I felt suddenly tired of them all—of Marietta, even of Iris. What did they think I was anyway, expecting me to work their miracles for them? The Virgin of Guadelupe? Marietta had gone off with her gun-toting citrus-grower. Why the hell hadn't she stayed with him? Why the hell did she have to come breaking into my house, submitting me to that final outrageous scene?

Marietta wasn't drinking her tequila. She was twisting the glass in her long hands.

"Aren't you going to ask me why I came?"

"I don't care," I said. "I'm past caring. I just figure this place has become a seminary for frustrated females and leave it at that."

"I'm sorry."

She sounded so doleful that it moved me. I crossed

and sat down at her side. I took her hand. After Sally, she was so nice to touch.

"Don't be sorry, Marietta. What happened? Where's your gunman?"

She looked up at me. Her eyes were dark. Suddenly she started to shiver.

"He wanted me to go home with him."

"No." I kidded her. "A man wanting to go home with you? I can't believe it."

"Those hands." She was shaking now like a thoroughbred terrier. "So big. Red hairs on the wrists."

The enigma of her had never been more tenebrous to me than at that moment. I thought of Sally's spat accusation that Marietta had made a fool of every man in Mexico. I thought of Marietta herself, calmly dating Jake to meet us in the Delta without telling me, calmly letting him maul her, calmly going with him when what he wanted was obvious. That fitted with my own conception of her—Marietta, the easy, cosmopolitan sophisticate. But here she was back on my hands, shaking, babbling of red hair on wrists, like a nun who had escaped violation by a pin's breath.

I kept her fingers in mine. I said, "Baby, do you English girls have to be told about life? Guys with red hair and fruit farms pick up girls in bars. They want the girls to go home with them. If the girls don't want to go home with them, they say no."

She tried to laugh, but her teeth were chattering. She said, "I'm a bloody fool. I know I'm a bloody fool. I'm sorry."

"Drink your tequila."

She lifted the glass with difficulty to her lips and drank. "I said no to him. I'm all right."

I was watching her, the way her hair came around her face, the trace of blue under her eyes like the veins in an iris, the wonderful curve of her lips.

"Marietta, tell me something. If you didn't want him, why did you let him take you away from the bar?"

"I don't know, Peter. I don't know about myself. Perhaps because you didn't want to go with me. Perhaps because I didn't want to be alone." She paused. "That's why I came back here—because I don't want to be alone to-night. Do you mind?"

I grinned. I held up my hands, letting the sleeves slip back. "No red hair on the wrists."

She smiled the sort of radiant smile that comes after tears, although she hadn't been crying. She leaned back against me, relaxing. There was a faint fragrance to her. I didn't know how cowslips smell, but it made me think of cowslips.

"It's all right when I'm with you, Peter. The jitters go. I don't know why. Perhaps because you're so big."

I said, "You're a problem child, too, aren't you? You and Sally."

"God," she said. "I hate problem children."

"Why don't you want to be alone? Is it Sally? Are you afraid of what she's going to do to-morrow?"

"Yes." She twisted around so that she was facing me. Her eyes were pleading. "Peter, can I sleep here to-night?"

"Carnally?"

"Don't be silly. You know you don't want that. I'll sleep on the couch in here. I'm used to sleeping on couches. When I lived with Martin, I always slept on a couch. There was only one bed."

"Which he took, of course."

"Of course."

Although she was being flippant again, I could trace the undercurrent of need. I had given up trying to understand her, but if she wanted to sleep on my couch it was okay with me.

I patted her arm and got up. "I guess you don't need pyjamas. I guess when you lived with Martin there was only one pair and he used them."

She smiled. "No. I'll take pyjamas."

I should have behaved like a gentleman and given her the bed, but I didn't. I'd lost my wife in Mexico. I could at least cling to my bed.

I got sheets, a pillow, and a blanket from the other room and a pair of cream-coloured pyjamas. She took the bedclothes and began gravely to spread them over the most un-bedlike Porfirio Díaz couch.

I went to her, put my hands on her arms. "Okay now?"

"Yes, thank you." She twisted around, looking at me, her lips half parted. "You must be horribly bored with me."

"You're difficult, not boring."

"You've been terribly kind."

"Don't be so British." I added, "You're not going to tell me what it is Sally has against you and Martin?"

She shook her head. "You'll know soon enough. Everyone will know."

"Maybe we can fix it yet," I said. "Maybe we'll think up something to-morrow."

Her whole body seemed to sag like a flower wilting.

"No," she said. "No, we won't think up anything. It's too late now."

She slid her hands up my arms. Her lips brushed mine. They were cool and soft. It was the first time we'd ever kissed.

"Good night, Peter. Try not to dream of Iris."

CHAPTER SIX

I didn't dream of anyone. I lay in my massive French bed, smoking cigarettes and thinking of women. For the last three weeks I had been smothered by women, confused by women's thinking, tugged at by women's desires, goaded by women's malice. I felt impregnated by femininity, like a cigarette from a woman's handbag tainted with the taste of face powder. I felt rebellious and muddled, because I didn't understand any of them. I didn't really understand Iris's tenacious desire to throw in her lot with Martin. I didn't understand Sally's demented desire to cling to a man who didn't want her. And, God knows, I didn't understand anything about Marietta. None of them operated the way a man would operate. They made no sense to me. I resented being sucked so profitlessly into their woman's world.

Through the tall French doors that led from the bedroom to the living room, light still fanned in. That meant Marietta wasn't asleep. She was probably lying there on the couch, smoking cigarettes, like me, and thinking. Of what? Of how to outwit Sally? No, that was too sensible and masculine. Probably she was shaking at the memory of red hairs on male wrists or yearning for Martin and the orchard on the home farm and the knobbly staffs made out of hawthorn.

I tried to believe in Sally's vicious threats. I tried to believe that to-morrow, probably, would be vastly and ominously different for all of them. But, for some reason, this feminine danger seemed less real than a scene in the cheapest movie. I wondered where Sally was now. Driving back to Taxco? She was the sort of crazy woman who would leap into a car and drive furiously through the night. I thought of the perilous road to Taxco, snaking through mountains, flanked with canyons. I thought of Sally with her little hands clutching the wheel of the automobile, her hair gleaming dead pale in the moonlight, her eyes bright with relentless malice. She had only to make one false movement of the wrist to plunge herself and the red convertible coupé into eternity.

I considered cold-bloodedly whether life would be better for me with Sally dead. It would be better for the others, obviously. Iris would get Martin. Martin would get money. Marietta would get freedom from the fear that haunted her. But what would I get?

Nothing, I decided. But then there was nothing for me anyway. I stubbed my cigarette.

Curiously enough, it was Sally I dreamed of and not Iris. Sally, thin and hot, pressed against me, her metal-heavy hair weighing me down, her lips, unyielding as metal, locked against mine.

I was awakened by sunlight splashing through the window which looked out on the green *patio*. I opened my eyes and remembered Marietta in the next room. I remembered too what the day had in store for us. I put on a bathrobe and went into the living room. The couch was restored to its normal stiff majesty. There was a neat pile of sheets and blankets on the floor at its side. Marietta wasn't there.

A piece of paper was propped against a lamp made out of a china blackamoor in pink lackey tights. I picked the note up. In Marietta's sprawling, oddly ingenuous handwriting was scribbled:

> Thanks, Peter. I'd have made breakfast for you if there'd been a kitchen and if I knew how to cook.
>
> Love,
MARIETTA.

If I'd been consistent, I'd have been relieved she had gone, but I wasn't. I felt hurt. This was a bad day for her. I'd expected her to need me as a sensible, enterprising male—someone to plan for her and decide how to ready herself for Sally's blow when it fell. I missed her too, and I felt uneasy. I hoped to hell she wasn't going to try some scatterbrained last-minute manœuvre.

I was shaving gloomily when the phone rang. Mexico has two competitive telephone systems. It always confused me. The wrong instrument always seemed to be ringing. This time I hit the right receiver on the first try. A Spanish voice said something which involved my name and Taxco. Then, like every other voice in Mexico, it said, *"momentito,"* which should mean a little moment but means anything up to half an hour.

This time I didn't have to wait long. I felt quite jittery, because Sally was the only person I knew in Taxco. It was Sally too. The pretty, light voice came across the wire, conciliatory with a faint bubbling of laughter behind it.

"Peter, did I wake you up?"

"Yes."

"I behaved awfully stupidly last night, didn't I?"

"Yes."

"I'm terribly sorry, really I am."

"That's why you're calling?"

"No. No, Peter. That isn't why I'm calling." Her voice sounded stronger, as if she was leaning into the mouthpiece. I could visualize the gold hair, shiny as the composition of the telephone, sliding around it. I could feel hair in my mouth. "Peter, I'm calling because of something terribly important."

"What?"

"Something you told me. Remember, Peter?" She laughed. It was a stilted laugh, almost as if she were drunk, but I didn't think she was. "Remember you called me a bitch, a nasty little spoiled rich bitch?"

"I guess I was a bit low, common, and vulgar."

"Oh, no. No. Not that. You were wonderful. I thought about it. All the way driving home I thought about it. I thought about how you said I should leave them alone— Martin and Marietta and Iris, how I was only trying to make them miserable to satisfy my own egoism. Remember?"

"Unfortunately I do."

"Don't say unfortunately, Peter. It's the truth. I've thought and it's the truth. Can I see you?"

"See me?"

"Yes, can you drive down to Taxco? It's only sixty

miles. You can come down." She laughed. "You aren't doing anything, anyway."

Incredibly, it seemed that losing my temper with her had been more effective than any crafty strategy I could have thought up. I said, "Sure I can come, Sally, if there's any point to my coming."

"Of course there's a point because—don't you see—I'm not going to the police to-day."

"You're not?"

"No." She paused. I could hear her breathing short, fluttery. The connection was that good. "Not to-day. Maybe I'll never go to the police if——"

"If?"

"If you come."

"Why do you want me?"

"Because. Because I want you to know what I know about them."

"About who?"

"About Martin and Marietta—what they did. I want you to know. I want you to advise me. If you think it's so bad I should go to the police, I'll go. If you think I should let them off, maybe I'll let them off."

I could hardly believe the Ericsson telephone. "And if I think you should let them off?"

"Maybe I will. Maybe I'll leave, Peter. Maybe I'll give Martin a divorce. Maybe I'll go back to the States. Maybe I'll go away."

"Okay, Sally. I'll be there. When?"

"Eight-thirty."

"Why so late?"

"I don't want you until eight-thirty."

"Okay."

"But you'll come?" Her voice was suddenly anxious. "You'll come?"

"Sure I'll come."

"I like you." She said that in a curious, quivery way. "I like the things you say to me. I like you."

Suddenly I saw her waiting for me at eight-thirty, waiting on a couch, maybe, smiling up at me with her small teeth, stretching the thin arms up, making the silver bracelets clatter. I'd been everything else for Iris. Did I have to be a stallion too?

I didn't say anything. Her voice sounded again sharply, "Peter, are you there?"

"Yes, I'm here."

"And you'll come?"

"Sure."

"Don't tell Marietta."

"No?"

"I don't want her to know I'm letting her off. I want her to sweat." She added with the beginning of anger in her voice, "She isn't there with you, is she?"

"No one's here. I'm alone."

"Then come."

"Eight-thirty."

"Eight-thirty. I like you."

There was the faintest suggestion of the giggle again. I heard her receiver click back on its stand.

CHAPTER SEVEN

I lit a cigarette, wondering about Sally. I contrasted ferocity of the night before with this new blandness. If I
hadn't known how unstable she was, I would have sus-
pected a trick, another turn of the screw. It might still be
a trick. And then again it might not. I knew I'd have to
go through with the Taxco trip. I'd set myself up as
everyone's little friend, the golden-hearted guy who
sorted out their problems. My own position was anoma-
lous, to say the least. If I did persuade Sally to give a
divorce, I lost Iris for good. But I also saved Marietta
from something very nasty.

Oddly enough, I was thinking mostly of Marietta.

She had never given me her address. That was part
of the enigma of her. But I had a telephone number. I
called it. Sally had said not to tell Marietta, but I didn't
let that worry me. She was just sitting there in Taxco
gloating over the thought of Marietta being frightened.
I had no sympathy with infantile sadists. At the telephone
number they told me Marietta was not there. They also
told me she hadn't been home all night. I knew that already. I was worried. I had a hunch that she was planning something foolish.

I finished shaving and went out. Everything was rinsed
in clean sunlight. My Indian was back with his peanuts.
To-day there were little scarlet rosettes of radishes too.
He had spread them on a sheet of yellow tissue paper.
It looked very gay. His whole stock could not have been
worth more than a dollar.

I walked to Sanborn's for breakfast. Sanborn's is where
the American tourists congregate over strawberry short-
cakes, bandying stomach conditions and bargains in
silver. The brassy normalcy of my compatriots was re-

55

freshing. To them Mexico wasn't a place where you lost your wife; it was something at the other end of Thomas Cook & Sons where you had to be careful about the water and where a lot of quaintness could be stored up on Kodachrome to bore the folks back home in Minnesota.

After breakfast I called Marietta again from an antiseptic booth near a rack of post-cards. She still wasn't there. I felt restless and I had nothing to do until it was time to start for Taxco. I wandered out into the narrow bustle of Madera. A little boy with silver watch chains slung like worms over his arm pursued me. Someone tried to sell me a puppy. An old man staggered past with a load of bird cages strapped on his back. The birds hopped around and whistled, brassy as the tourists. I like Mexican streets. The small things that happen on them have so much vitality.

I strolled down San Juan de Letran and made my way home past the San Juan Market, wandering through the flower stalls opulent with roses, scarlet carnations, tuberoses, lilac stock, and tall blue spider lilies. I had hoped to find Marietta at home or some word from her, but there was nothing.

The futility of my life in Mexico City was never more apparent to me than on that morning. I had nothing to do. I knew no one except Marietta and wanted to know no one. In contrast to this nothingness, the trip to Taxco seemed almost inviting. At least it was something definite to do. I called Marietta again. They told me she had come in with an American man and gone out almost immediately, saying she would not be back until the next day. She'd left no message for me. I asked what the American man looked like. They said he was big and redheaded.

The news staggered me. Last night Marietta had been shivering with disgust at Jake. This morning she had left my apartment and gone straight to him. I felt a frustrated indignation. I felt anxious too. Where was she going with her dubious citrus-grower? To Taxco?

Urgency came on me. I went to the garage for my car. I'd reach Taxco too early for my date with Sally. That didn't matter. I wanted to be there. It seemed important now.

I swung up into the mountains, dust-brown and parched from the lack of rain. At startling intervals, the two great volcanoes that brood over Mexico slid in and out of view, Popocatepetl's snow-lonely peak, the Sleeping Woman, quiet and ominous with a scarf of cloud. A single Indian led a burro loaded with taffy cornhusks. A yellow butterfly flapped nowhere. There was nothing else. Up here the whole world seemed empty.

In Mexico, climate isn't north and south. It's up and down. I toppled from barren highland into sudden valleys lush with chartreuse sugar cane and the cool jade of bananas. I had lunch in Cuernavaca in a *patio* that was hot with bougainvillæa amid carnations. Twenty minutes later I was up again in the barren cactus highlands.

I was making good time until I got a flat between Cuernavaca and Xoxocotla. After that, it was hell. I had no jack. It had been stolen in Mexico. I had to thumb a ride back to Cuernavaca and dicker with a lethargic garage. It was quarter to six before I was on my way again. There was still time to keep my date with Sally, but I was unreasonably anxious about Marietta. If I'd understood her, I wouldn't have been worried. But I didn't understand her, and because I didn't understand her I imagined her capable of the most foolhardy things.

The evening was a faded pink when a twist in the road brought Taxco into view. Clinging to the mountainside with its weathered red roofs and its twin-steepled cathedral frothy as meringue, it is to me one of the most beautiful towns on this continent. That night the very air seemed rose-coloured from the sunset. It wasn't a town; it was a spray of peach blossom.

I thought of Sally sitting in it, waiting for me, like a little yellow spider with its web spun between the blossoms.

I turned into the street which led into the town. It was cobbled, steep, narrow, never meant for an automobile. I'd been in Taxco six years before, but Sally hadn't been there then. I didn't know where she lived. It was eight-fifteen. There was no time to try to find out whether Marietta and Jake were there. I parked in a side street below the Zocalo, next to a dilapidated burro and a tethered turkey. Two small pigs liked it. They came squealing out of a doorway and, squeezing underneath the car, collapsed into sleep.

From the Zocalo above me, wheezy steam-organ music blared down through the thickening twilight. Some church fiesta must have been getting under way. An Indian with a red-and-grey serape started coping with the pigs. I asked him where the Señora Haven lived. Everyone knows everything about everyone in Taxco. He pointed up the hill to a higher church. It was near there. The next house above the church.

I started on foot up the cobbled street. It was impossible to take the car any farther. The street was so steep that I had to lean forward to keep my balance. Apart from an old, old woman with an empty kerosene can, the place was deserted. Everyone must already have congregated in the public square.

I reached the church which clung precariously to the mountainside. A footpath wound upward past its pink walls. Chickens scurried out of my way. A pig lumbered toward the church door. The path swerved right, and there was Sally's house, new looking and rich, spread across the hill above the town.

I passed through iron gates and up a twisting driveway, sombre with the heavy green of bananas. I came to a flagged area with a tiled pool full of showy goldfish. The front door was beyond it. It was open. I moved to it, hesitated on the threshold, looking for a buzzer to ring. I couldn't see one. It was exactly eight-thirty. I called, "Sally," tapped on the door, and walked in.

I was in the living-room, a huge, tall room glowing with the pale colours of modern Mexican furniture. The air was dusky, and no lights had been lit. A girl was crouched in a chair near the window. I assumed it was Sally because I was expecting her.

I went toward her, saying, "Hello, Sally."

She stirred. Her hair was dark. No trick of light could make Sally's metal hair that dark. With disproportionate anxiety, I thought it was Marietta sitting there alone in Sally's living-room.

The girl got up then. She stood silhouetted against the tall windows. I crossed to her through the puzzling half-light. I was almost at her side before I recognized her. It seemed incredible to me that I could have been in a room with her and not known her. It was just that the possibility of her being there had been so remote. For a second the muscles of my legs felt thin as water.

"Iris," I said.

CHAPTER EIGHT

She wore her coat slung over her shoulders, Sally-style. Her dark hair gleamed in the pink light that was hardly light. Her face was thin and terribly pale. She looked as if she had been sick for weeks. I wondered if her idyll with Martin was doing this to her.

She stared at me, her eyes almost vacant. I was surprised that seeing me should be such a shock. And I'd been thinking about her so much that I had lost the faculty of being natural. I felt awkward, clumsy.

"Peter." Her hand came out and took my sleeve. Even the touch of her hand was different. That wasn't the way my wife's fingers had felt. "Peter, I didn't recognize you. So dark."

She seemed to be making a terrific effort at control. I said, "What are you doing here?"

"Me?" She paused as if thinking what she was doing there. Then the words came hurriedly. "Sally sent for me. She called me in Acapulco. She said not to tell Martin, but she wanted to talk to me. She said maybe—maybe everything could be arranged." She added, "And you?"

"Remember your SOS? I'm here to talk to Sally too. Where is she?"

Iris leaned against the arm of a sofa that glowed a pale yellow. "I don't know. I just came. I knocked on the door. Nothing happened. The door was open. I walked in. She isn't here."

"And the servants?"

"There's some kind of fiesta. She must have let them all go to the fiesta."

A flat silence came. We stood there in the gloom close together but like strangers—worse than strangers, because there was that quivering tension between us.

60

I said stiffly, in a tea-party voice, "I hope you are well."

"Yes, thank you, Peter."

"And Martin?"

"He's well too. He doesn't know I'm here."

I stared down at the carpet. Some small object gleamed dully. I tried to identify it. A slipper? Yes, a silver slipper sprawled on its side. Beyond it, over by the open French windows leading to the terrace, a big vase full of tuberoses had fallen off a table and was lying on the carpet. I wondered if the wind had knocked it down.

"I hope you're happy," I said.

"Yes, Peter, yes." The words sprang from her.

There seemed so much bravado that my heart melted for her. I didn't mind any more that she was shutting me out. I went to her. I put my hands on her arms. She was shivering the way Marietta had shivered. Because what had happened between us had made me physically humble, I thought she found my touch repulsive. I took my hands away.

"Iris," I said, "I want things to turn out right for you. You believe that, don't you?"

She didn't answer.

I said, "On the phone Sally told me too that things might be arranged. Maybe she was telling the truth. Maybe it'll pan out."

"Don't, please," she whispered.

"Iris, baby, what's the matter?"

She threw herself against me, sliding her arms around me. "Let's get away from here. This room, I hate it. Don't let's wait. Please, Peter, let's go."

I was exhilarated because she was in my arms of her own accord. That meant more to me than the desperation in her.

I said quietly, "Don't be silly, baby. This is important. We've got to wait. Maybe between us, we can——"

I heard footsteps at the door behind me. Then a reading lamp was snapped on. Iris broke from my arms. I turned to face the door, expecting Sally.

It wasn't Sally. Large and handsomely brash in his tight gaberdine suit, Jake Lord stood on the threshold. Under the cropped red hair he was grinning at me.

"Well, well," he said. "Pardon *me*."

We both stared at him, uncertain. He strolled into the room throwing a casual glance around its muted elegancies.

"Well," he said again. "Fancy finding you here, Peter." He came very close to us, staring blatantly at Iris. "And the little lady?"

I said, "Iris, this is Jake Lord. Jake—my wife."

"Your wife?" He gave me the sort of wink that is associated with travelling-salesmen stories and hitched up his pants over his lean stomach. "Well, we live and learn."

His self-assurance was impertinent and faintly ominous. He lounged away from us through the room. There was a desk with a typewriter and a sheet of paper in it. He paused, looking down shamelessly, reading what was written.

He glanced back at me. "Marietta here?"

"Marietta?"

He flicked a cigarette out of his pocket and lit it. "Yeah. This house belongs to a party called Mrs. Sally Haven, doesn't it?"

"Yes," I said.

He dropped into a chair, inhaling deeply, watching Iris as if she was a juicy number at a taxi-dance joint. "Sure Marietta isn't here, Peter?"

"Why should she be?"

He shrugged the wrestler's shoulders. "Here's where she said she was coming. She's crazy, that one, dragged me out of bed, told me I had to drive her to Taxco. Seems there was something she had to fix with this Haven dame. She's her sister-in-law, isn't she?"

"Yes," I said, feeling uneasy.

"Came up here a couple of hours ago. Left me stuck in a bar down town. I figured a couple of hours was long enough for any two girls to jabber at each other." He threw out his big hands. "Here I am."

I said, "If Marietta was here, she's gone. You must have passed her."

"Yeah? And this Sally Haven?"

"She's not here either."

He grinned at me. "Just you and your wife, eh? Hope I'm not intruding."

"Why should you be?"

He started to whistle. He got up, glanced down at the silver slipper, and kicked at it with his toe. His sharp blue eyes moved to the white, overturned tuberoses.

"Does she carry liquor, this dame? I'm dry as Arizona."

Iris was sitting very pale and stiff in a chair. Jake moved past her, so close that his arm brushed her. He paused, looking down at her curiously.

"My, little lady, you look peaked. Maybe she's got a bar on the terrace. Come on. I'll rustle up a little of what ails you."

He bent over her and, taking her arms, lifted her to her feet. I pushed him away from her. He grinned his grin with the blue eyes wide open. "Now don't get sore, Peter. No offence intended." He put his hand on Iris's sleeve. "Just offering the little lady a little snort."

He started toward the French windows to the terrace. Iris recoiled from him to me. He disappeared. Iris and I followed, for no particular reason unless we were trying to avoid being alone.

The terrace was wide and white and long. It stretched the length of the house with a precipitous view of Taxco over a white-painted wooden balustrade. The lights were on now. They twinkled down the hillside like silver chains connected to the major brightness of the Zocalo. Santa Prisca had been dressed up for the fiesta. Strings of lights were strewed across its massive façade, and high up, between the twin steeples, sparkled a great Star of Bethlehem.

Carrousel music drifted to us on the still night air. Jake was moving away from us down the terrace, peering for liquor. A small polished moon hung almost directly above us, adding its milk-blue radiance to the fiesta. Iris stood very close to me, taut, staring down the plunging view at the quivering beauty of the town.

The carrousel was wheezing out "La Barca de Oro." From far down the terrace, Jake started to whistle the ever-popular song along with the music. Suddenly his whistle stopped. For a second the terrace was quiet as an abandoned church. Then Jake's voice came, strange, harsh.

"Hey, Peter, hey, you girl, come here."

I started toward him. Iris hesitated and then, coming after me, slipped her cold hand into mine. We passed low, shadowy porch chairs and divans. Jake's large figure loomed ahead. He was standing with his back to us, peering down over the balustrade. And, as we drew closer, I saw that there was no balustrade there. Part of it had broken off, leaving a gaping hole.

We reached him. Down in the Zocalo the steampipes of the carrousel were sobbing. The words of the song were so familiar to me that they jogged along with the music in my mind.

> *"Voy a aumentar los mares con me llanto*
> *Adiós, mujer . . ."*

Jake heard us coming. He turned sharply. In the moonlight his face was utterly changed. The blandness was gone. He looked grim and tough as a gun. He grabbed my arm. He pulled me toward the gap in the balustrade. Beyond it there was a sheer drop of over thirty feet into a dry, rocky stream bed.

"Get a load of that, Peter," he said.

I saw it, of course. First I saw the strip of broken balustrade where it had fallen. Then I saw the hair—hair gleaming, metallic, almost white in the moonlight. I saw the hair and I saw the little white hands, flung up. I saw the tiny body sprawled there below on the jagged rocks—limp as a doll tossed away by a bored child.

The words of the song were still pounding in my ears, running with the carrousel music.

> *"Adiós, mujer, adiós para siempre adiós."*

The parallel between the mournful words and the thing below made me feel sick.

Jake said, "She's as dead a dame as I'd care to see. Back's broken; you can tell from the position. Who is it? Mrs. Haven?"

I became conscious of Iris then. She sagged against

me, and her voice rose, shrill, jagged, over the lamenting music.

"She was lying there all the time. Sally was lying there and I didn't know."

At first that remark, wrenched out of her, seemed completely without sense to me. Why should she say she hadn't known Sally was lying there? Of course she hadn't known Sally was lying there.

Slowly Jake turned to her. His eyes were bright in the moonlight.

"You didn't know it, eh?"

"I didn't," said Iris. "I didn't. I didn't."

The hysteria of that repetition was bad enough. But suddenly I felt as if Sally's terrace was dissolving beneath my feet.

Iris was my wife. I had loved her for five years. I knew every in and out of her mind, every inflection of her voice.

And I knew then that her voice was false. She was lying. She had known Sally was there.

All the time she had been with me, in the living-room, she had known that Sally was lying there—dead.

CHAPTER NINE

I led Iris to one of the porch chairs. I made her sit. I said, "Jake and I've got to go down to Sally."

I didn't know if she was listening. She had folded her hands and was looking at a ring on her finger. It was a new ring. From Martin? In the darkness her face was white as the tuberoses scattered behind her. I was scared of what she might say or do. I leaned down and whispered like a conspirator, "Be careful. For God's sake, be careful."

Jake had swung himself down through the gap in the balustrade. I hurried after him. Jake with his gun, his swaggering impudence, his possible connection with Sally, was an unknown quantity. He was bright, I knew. He was also potentially hostile. I couldn't afford to have him discover whatever there might be to discover without my being there.

When I formulated that thought, I didn't let myself admit what it implied.

The drop to the dry stream bed was almost sheer. I started clambering after Jake, clinging to jutting stones and crevices. He had reached the stream bed and was bending over Sally. I joined him. The edge of the broken segment of balustrade was lying over her legs. Jake pushed it aside. I noticed at once that one of the little feet was bare. On the other, a silver slipper gleamed.

The moonlight was strong, blue like the moonlight in Swan Lake. The slight body seemed to have no substance. The metal hair poured over a rock. Her eyes were open. They stared up at nothing. Her lips were parted too. I could see the white teeth. There was no blood. But the position of the body told the story. A

66

body couldn't be hunched backward that way unless the spine was shattered.

I took her thin, cold wrist with its sagging silver bracelets.

There was no pulse.

Jake was squatting at my side. His thigh brushed against mine, solid and warm and in violent contrast to the chill of that dead wrist.

"Well," he said.

As we crouched there, Sally's voice, light and pretty with its suppressed giggle, seemed to weave in my mind with the music from the Zocalo. *Peter, I like you.* I shivered. *Maybe I'll never go to the police—if you come.* She'd said that. She'd changed her mind. Marietta might have been saved from jail. Martin might have got his divorce. Iris might have got Martin.

Everything might have been all right—without this.

My hand moved from her wrist up her arm. Jake pushed it roughly away.

"Don't touch. Mexican law's death on touching." He paused. "Back broken, eh?"

"Yes."

He got up, flexing the muscles of his legs. His steady eyes considered the gaping hole in the balustrade above us.

"Must have leaned against it and it gave way."

"Yes."

As I said that, a thought splashed through my mind like acid. The broken strip of balustrade had been lying across Sally's legs. If she'd leaned against the balustrade and it had given way, it would have reached the ground before her. It could never have landed on her legs.

It couldn't have happened that way.

I thought of Iris above us, hunched in the porch chair, and I felt a kind of despair. Sooner or later Jake would realize about the balustrade. He'd remember when he looked back, because he was the one who had pulled the broken wood off Sally.

We stood there, over the little body, both big men, watching each other.

"Yeah," he said almost casually. "She was alone on

the terrace; she leaned against the balustrade, maybe admiring the view—and the balustrade gave way."

"I guess so," I said, hardly believing he could be that unobservant.

"Sure. That's the way it was." He thrust his hands into his pockets. "Well, guess there's nothing more we can do down here. Better call the police, eh?"

"Yes."

He started swinging himself up toward the terrace. I followed. His legs dangled in my face. I looked back once, and the metal hair still gleamed down there in the moonlight.

On the balcony, Iris was standing, the coat on her shoulders, gazing down at the sparkle of Taxco below. She was smoking a cigarette. The carnival sounds trailed up, the moan of the pipe organ and the dry whirring of the revolving carrousel.

When she turned, I knew she had got a grip on herself.

She asked quickly, "Is she dead?"

I could trace the aritificiality of her voice, but it was steady—steady enough, I hoped, to fool a stranger.

"I'm afraid so, Iris."

Jake laid a hand on her shoulder.

"What d'you know? We come calling on a dame and she has to fall off of a balcony. And with no liquor in the house. What sort of hospitality is that?"

The facetiousness grated, but I supposed that was his idea of easing the tension.

Iris asked, "The police?"

"Yeah. We're going to call them now."

"I hope someone speaks English," I said.

"Spanish not so good, Peter?" Jake shrugged. "Don't you worry. No, sir. These spick lingoes don't bother me. Just relax. Uncle Jake takes over from now on."

He started through the French windows into the lighted living-room. For a couple of bleak moments Iris and I stayed together on the terrace. I was half hoping, half dreading she would confide in me. But she didn't. We went on into the living-room. We found Jake looking down at the spilled vase of tuberoses on the yellow carpet. With a little cluck, he bent and replaced the vase on its table. He wiped the wet patch on the carpet with his handkerchief.

"Sloppy dame," he murmured.

He moved into the centre of the room. His eyes darted about. They fell on the silver slipper sprawled near the couch. He began to whistle hissingly through his teeth, no particular tune.

"Leaving her slippers all over the place. Anyone'd think she was tight." His bright eyes fixed my face with a glance that was strangely intimate. "Know what these Mexican cops'll think when they see that slipper?"

Iris, close to me, was trembling. I knew what I was thinking. *Why should Sally have kicked one slipper off in the living-room before she—accidentally—fell off the balcony?*

I had a sudden gnawing vision of Sally and Iris struggling in that elegant pastel living-room, a vision of Sally's slipper being kicked off, of the vase of tuberoses being overturned, a vision of the struggle moving out on to the balcony, of Sally's little body being pushed back against the balustrade. I felt sweat breaking out on my forehead. I glanced at Iris. Her face was expressionless as an idol's, except for the eyes. They were eyes looking at a guillotine.

Jake's question still seemed to hang in the air.

Trying to sound dumb, I asked. "What'll they think, Jake?"

He didn't answer at once. It was almost as if he knew he was keeping me in suspense and enjoying it. Then he grinned suddenly.

"They'll think she was plastered. That's what they'll think." He bent and picked up the slipper, letting it dangle. "You know Jake. Always chivalrous. Least we can do is to protect the little lady's reputation."

While I watched incredulously, he moved back on to the balcony. He strolled its length and tossed the slipper down through the brooked gap in the balustrade. He came back, rubbing his hands together.

"It'd have been a shame," he said, "letting these Mexicans think something so indelicate." The grin moved to Iris's white face. "Don't look so scared, baby. No one's going to eat you. Now for the cops."

He went toward the telephone. To reach it, he had to pass the desk where the portable typewriter stood with the sheet of paper in it. He had started to whistle again. As he came to the table, he looked at the typewriter, stopped whistling, pulled the paper out of the roller, and folded it into his pocket. Then he resumed the monotonous whistle and picked up the telephone.

It was that final act of slipping the paper into his pocket which made me realize what he had been doing from the start. It had been Jake who removed the broken balustrade from its damaging position on top of Sally's legs. It had been Jake who had returned the vase of tuberoses to the table. It had been Jake who had tossed the silver slipper down beside Sally's body. And now it was Jake who had pulled the paper—I didn't know what paper—from the typewriter.

He knew as well as Iris and I that Sally had not died by accident. And yet, for some reason, he was not an enemy. He was systematically and efficiently removing all questionable evidence before he called the police.

He was still holding the telephone, but he had not picked up the receiver. His leisurely gaze was moving around the room. At length it settled on me.

"Uncle Jake's been thinking," he said. "You don't know Mexicans. Suspicious race. Can be pretty devious, jumping at conclusions, twisting things. Now Iris came here alone. Peter came here alone. I came here alone. That's kind of complicated, isn't it? Something that might give a wrong impression."

I took Iris's arm to steady her. "And what do you suggest?"

The white teeth flashed. "A little simplification. That's what I like. Simple things. No one saw me coming up that dark alley. And you?"

"There was an old woman farther down by the church, that's all."

We both turned to Iris. She was looking at Jake, her mouth tight at the corners. "Everyone was at the fiesta," she said.

Jake nodded, contented. "Okay, so it's a cinch. Peter and Iris and me, we're friends, see? We all had a drink down town and thought it'd be fun to drop up and visit

Mrs. Haven. We all came in a bunch—and found her down there where she'd fallen through the rotten balustrade. That what we did, isn't it?"

There was no doubt now. He had come out in the open. I hadn't the faintest idea what was behind it all, but he was saying, *You play along with me and I'll play along with you and everything will be okay.*

The luck seemed too good to be true. I said, "Sure, Jake. I think you've got something there."

"Of course I have. Jake always has something there." He took the receiver off the hook and started talking in calm, unrattled Spanish.

I assumed he was asking the operator for the police, but I didn't have much time to think about it because Iris had fainted.

CHAPTER TEN

I picked Iris up and carried her to the yellow couch. I was almost sure she had fainted from relief. She had been terrified of Jake, terrified of the police. Then miraculously Jake had become an ally and it had been too much for her.

I laid her down on the couch and took one of her unresisting hands. I realized that this was the hand which had been wearing the new ring. The ring was not there.

I glanced down and saw it lying on the carpet at my feet. I picked it up. It had obviously been too big for her finger and must have slipped off. It was a gold ring with no jewel, more like a man's ring, with a plaited gold band and a shield of gold decorated with tiny heraldic lions. It made me think of Martin. I put it in my pocket, out of sight.

Jake had finished telephoning. He strolled across to me. I got up and joined him. He looked at Iris.

"Couldn't take it, eh, Peter?"

"It's the reaction."

"Sure." He squatted on the arm of a chair, tugging at his pants, exposing a big chunk of calf. "Women are strange. They're the most hard-boiled animal ever created. Then suddenly they fold."

He lit a cigarette with a heavy silver lighter. He stared over the flame at the low neck of Iris's dress. "Well, I called the cops. They'll be right up. Or as right up as a Mexican policeman chooses to come when there's a fiesta."

I thought of some odd little police station down there on the cobbled streets below us. I thought of policemen with skin brown as honey hurrying out into the music-loud darkness. It seemed almost impossible that our des-

tinies hung now on those unknown men, so exotic, so removed from our lives.

"What did you tell them?"

"That there'd been an accident. That Mrs. Haven was
dead. They knew Mrs. Haven."

He sat there, heavy, handsome, positive of the simplicity of what lay ahead.

I said, "You're pretty sure there'll be no trouble, aren't
you?"

"Trouble?" He shrugged. "Where's there any trouble
about a dame falling off her own balcony?"

"There's a lot more to this than you know."

He opened the blue eyes wide. "There is?"

I disliked having to strip myself in front of this man
whom I didn't understand or like. But already I was
hopelessly entangled with him, subtly dependent upon
him too—if only because he could speak Sapnish and
would have to be the spokesman.

I said, "Sally's husband is in love with my wife. He
left her. He's been trying to get a divorce. Sally wouldn't
give it to him. Everyone in Taxco knows it."

"So." Jake blew a smoke ring. His eyes moved slowly
over me and then shifted to Iris. "A domestic drama."

"If you like."

"What's his name—this guy? Sally's husband?"

"Martin Haven."

"Must have a lot on the ball."

"That's not the point right now."

"And what is the point?" He was smiling with that
amused naïveté which he cultivated and which I found
somehow ominous. He never accepted an overtone. He
committed you to saying what you were thinking.
"What's worrying you, Peter?"

"People will say Sally died at a convenient time for
Martin and Iris."

He blinked. "Big-hearted, aren't you? Worrying about
a dame who threw you over for another man."

"It doesn't matter, what I am," I said.

"Well, well." He looked down at the carpet and then
up at me with mock solemnity. "Maybe we were wrong
about the way Sally died. Maybe it wasn't an accident."
The grin came again. "That poor kid. She loved her

73

husband. She'd lost him to another girl. There she was alone with no hope of getting her man back, with no one to turn to. Life didn't seem worth living any more. An impulse came. She was half crazy with unhappiness." He threw out his hands. "She tossed herself through the balustrade. Suicide."

The idea of Sally in the role of the broken blossom killing herself for unrequited love was preposterous to me, of course. But would it be preposterous to everyone?

Jake leaned forward, balanced on the chair arm, his big hands on his massive knees. "We don't mention that at first, of course. It's an accident. That's what we say. But then if things don't pan out, if they start asking awkward questions, we kind of shuffle and look uncomfortable and let them dope it out that we suspect she killed herself, but are too gentlemanly to say so." One of the hands came forward and touched my arm. I noticed the red hairs on the thick wrist. "How's about that, Peter?"

I saw that we might just get away with it if we played it right. But that the suggestion should have come from him was the fantastic climax of his fantastic behaviour. My need to know his motives was stronger than my discretion, and I said, "Why in hell are you doing this?"

"Doing what, Peter?" The old naïve smile was back. "I don't have to tell you that."

"But you do, Peter. What d'you think I am? One of those dames with earrings and a crystal ball?"

"Why are you suppressing evidence? Why are you faking these stories for the police that aren't true?"

"Aren't true, Peter?" He got up and moved to my side, putting his arm heavily on my shoulder. He had to touch you whether you were male or female. "That's making it kind of elaborate, isn't it? I'm just simplifying, making things easier."

"But why bother? What's in it for you?"

He took his arm off my shoulder. He looked hurt. "Why's there got to be anything in it for me? A pal helps out a pal, don't he?"

"But you don't know Iris. You hardly know me."

"Maybe I make friends quick." He flicked his cigarette butt into a tray. "Sure you're my pal, Peter. And Marietta's my pal too. Remember?" The blue eyes showed a gleam that seemed faintly derisive. "Marietta was here tonight too. I'd do a lot for Marietta."

That was the explanation he was handing out. He was doing all this for Marietta.

Iris stirred on the couch. I hurried to her. The lashes flickered. Her eyes opened.

"Peter."

I dropped to my knees at her side. She smiled her warm, natural smile she used to give me when she loved me. Then the smile went, crowded out by memory of where she was and what had happened, and she was a stranger again.

Jake had crossed to my side. Iris's gaze moved to him. "You called the police?"

"Sure thing, baby."

"And you're going to talk to them?"

"Don't you worry your pretty little head. I'm going to talk to them. And you're not."

"I'm not?"

Jake squatted down next to me and took her hand. "You've had a big shock, baby. You're confused. You can't talk straight. You're not worth wasting the cops' valuable time on. Know where you're going? You're going to bye-bye in the bedroom."

He lifted her off the couch, one big arm around her back, the other sliding behind her knees, the fingers resting on the tan silk of her stocking.

"Prostrated by shock, baby. That's what you are. Lying on the bed, prostrated by shock. You don't know a thing, anyways. It was Peter and me who found the body. Remember? You were never out on the terrace."

He held her close so that her cheek was touching his. He carried her away into the bedroom. When he turned, there was a knock on the door.

Feeling terrible, I opened it.

The police had arrived.

There were three of them. They were all young and solemn and small and beautiful in the dazed, swimming-eyed fashion of the young Indian. They were also very polite. They wore uniforms which were snappy but slightly too large for them, as if they were still growing

75

and an economical Government was making allowance for that fact.

What I had expected to be an ordeal wasn't an ordeal at all. Jake, very candid and friendly, took complete charge. He talked in fluent, rapid Spanish and one or another of them would break in with a soft, almost singing question. The slightly older one who seemed to be in charge took copious notes in a small book, writing determinedly with a scrap of pink tongue tucked over the dark lower lip like a schoolchild taking dictation. They made no attempt to see Iris and paid me scarcely any attention. Every once in a while, when my name came into the dialogue, one of them would shoot me a rather shy smile as if apologizing for talking about me in a language I couldn't understand. I had had a preconceived idea of Mexican officials as strutting, self-important martinets. These policemen weren't that way at all.

Jake took them out on the terrace. They were gone quite a long time, but I did not join them. I felt at the moment I could do no good, only harm. When they returned, the dialogue continued. They must have asked a great many questions about Sally's personal life and personal habits, but Jake never appealed to me for information. He must have been putting on a colossal bluff.

It was maddening to be so in need of knowledge as to what was going on and yet be completely incapable of understanding a single phrase. I kept the three pairs of smoky, long-lashed eyes under constant observation, trying to catch a change of expression. But they remained smiling, polite, almost sympathetic.

At last Jake said something and turned to me. "Peter, come into the bedroom a moment, will you?"

The three policemen were watching me. They nodded to show that I had their permission. They smiled too— three white, sudden smiles.

I followed Jake into the bedroom. Iris, lying on the bed, sat up, pushing the hair back from her face, watching us. She had put on lipstick, and the full scarlet of her lips emphasized the whiteness of her skin.

I said, "Well?"

Jake grinned broadly and, clasping his hands together, brandished them over his head like a champion boxer.

"The winnah!"

"Tell us," I said.

"They're sure it's an accident. One of them's uncle's the carpenter who built the building in the first place. Seems Mrs. Haven complained to him only a week ago that the balcony was rotten and dangerous. He was supposed to have come and fixed it. He didn't come—being Mexican. And his nephew feels kind of guilty, feels the old man's responsible. He's the Captain of Police too. Boy, what a break!" The blue eyes were frankly triumphant. "Unless something unexpected happens, there's not going to be any trouble. One of the other kids' father's the town undertaker. I've promised him the business for poppa. He's going to take care of the body. I'm to hang around and supervise. We're to notify the husband too. There'll be an inquest. To-morrow, maybe. But if the graft in this town is up to the graft in Mexico City, it's in the bag. The Captain's going to keep uncle's nose clean. I'm going to keep very quiet about the uncle, too. Americans aren't human beings to them, anyway. They're just crazy things with bank rolls and crazy habits. If one dies, it's about as important as if a duck-billed platypus died."

His buoyant optimism was such that I couldn't help being affected by it. It no longer seemed strange that, tacitly, he and Iris and I were banded together to deceive the law. It had become a violently personal issue in which it would be fatal to lose.

And right now we seemed to be winning.

Jake had sat down on the bed, balancing himself by a hand on Iris's knee. "One thing, Peter. In Mexico there's a custom. There's the same custom in the States, only it's more under the counter back home."

"The custom?"

"In the States, you buy the Chief of Police a new automobile." He shrugged. "Here, when a policeman's nice to you, you're nice to him. Got any money?"

I took out my wallet. I had a hundred-peso bill and two fifties. I wondered how much it cost to buy freedom. I offered him the bills. He laughed.

"Keep your dough. They're all on a starvation wage.

Fifty's plenty for the three of the poor devils. It's more than they've seen in months."

That's how much it cost. Fifty pesos for the three. Three dollars and thirty-three cents each.

Iris was leaning forward, her dark hair falling over her face.

Jake took the bill and nodded to me to follow him to the living-room. The three policemen were still standing in a line, smiling.

Jake handed the bill to the Captain. He took it without the faintest trace of embarrassment. The three white grins grew broader.

Jake said something and then turned to me. "There's no need for you to stick around. They say you can leave if the lady's well enough to travel.

I couldn't believe it was being as easy as this, but it was.

"Where you staying?" asked Jake.

I hadn't planned to spend the night in Taxco, of course. I said, "Nowhere right now."

"Get rooms at that big hotel as you enter town. The Borda. Get me one too. I'll join you later. Let you know about the inquest to-morrow, the works."

"Okay," I said.

He paused and then added softly, "And for God's sake, before you do anything else, locate Marietta."

Marietta.

"Try the bars," he said. "If I know that dame, it's the bars."

He patted my arm, like an indulgent father, although he must have been a couple of years younger than I. "Run along now, Peter. Scram."

I went into the bedroom for Iris. I said, "It's okay. We're leaving."

CHAPTER ELEVEN

Out of the house, the high mountain air was sweet. Below us, the papier-mâché Star of Behtlehem hung glistening like a portent between the church's twin steeples. The music, seeping up from the Zocalo, seemed part of the moonlight.

On the toppling descent past the dark, secondary church, past the unlit houses where begonias gleamed white on high balconies, Iris kept as far from me as possible, avoiding a chance physical contact from a stumble on the cobblestones. Her wary silence became unendurable, particularly now when the first confusions were gone and I had started to realize to the full the huge change Sally's death would make for all of us.

We took a twist in the road, past a pig grunting in its sleep by a heap of straw. The coloured lights and the glossy-leaved trees of the Zocalo shone below us like a stomacher.

"Martin won't need a divorce now," I said.

"No."

"And you'll marry him?"

She whispered, "Yes, I'll marry him."

"We'd better call him in Acapulco. Let him know."

Iris pulled the coat around her as if she was cold. "Yes, we'd better call him."

"He doesn't know you're here, does he?"

"No," she said stiffly, making it clear she had nothing more to say to me.

We dropped into a narrow street like a funnel and suddenly we were in the plaza. It was a change as violent as stepping from midnight into high noon. The little park inside the frame of dark trees was ablaze with colour, stalls bright with candied fruit and trashy toys, a rickety

79

bingo stand, a pink children's swing, and the carrousel with golden horses, sad and peeling. Indians swarmed everywhere; so did dogs and pigs and turkeys. Children stared longing-eyed at posts decorated with flambeaux of spun-sugar candy. And the cathedral, grey-pink behind its frivolous strings of lights, seemed to be dancing in the air.

The hurdy-gurdy music made the square shrill. It mingled with the human noises, the laughter, the shouts, the squabbles. This near, the roar of the revolving carrousel was like the stampede of an army in flight.

I said, "We've got to find Marietta. You don't know her, do you?"

"No."

"She's probably in a bar, Jake said. We'd better go to Paco's. It's up there on the balcony across from the cathedral. I remember. That's where most foreigners go."

Now that Iris had shut me out, I was thinking of Marietta with a kind of excited anxiety. Marietta belonged with fiesta, with coloured lights and the pink children's swing. Marietta would have bought a stick of pink foamy candy and eaten it with the grave relish of an Indian child. Marietta would have ridden on the carrousel, unsmiling, remote, lost in a dream, but part of the carnival.

Marietta who had come to me last night, whose cool kiss had asked me to forget Iris. Marietta, haunted by furies, who had made Jake drive her to Taxco to see Sally.

Why?

I took Iris's arm and guided her past the carrousel in the direction of Paco's. She seemed as remote to me now, with my thoughts of Marietta, as I had been to her. I almost resented her for monopolizing all my emotion when Marietta too might be caught in the invisible web that had been spun at the Casa Haven.

The organ sobbed into "Begin the Beguine," which, here south of the border, sounded Manhattan as the Stork Club. The carrousel lumbered around and around. Two little girls were crouched together on a sombre gold horse, their faces white with ecstasy, their pigtails streaming behind them. A very thin old Indian with a scarlet serape lumbered around straight as an angry cat's tail. A girl giggled by, waving to a couple of youths in slick, American suits. Then I stopped dead, staring.

I had seen him first as a gleam of yellow coming around on the carrousel, a gleam of yellow hair startlingly out of place behind the glossy black hair of the Mexican riding the horse in front of him. He swung round into full view. He was riding the gold horse lightly as if it were a hunter. He looked about eighteen. His skin was golden from the sun, darker than his hair. A yellow balloon bobbed on a string from his left hand. He was grave, absorbed with the infantile pleasure of circular motion—just as Marietta would have been.

Iris had stopped dead too.

"Martin."

I turned to her and her face was so stripped that I looked away.

The carrousel started to slow down, losing its synchronization with "Begin the Beguine." The two little girls, tittering daringly, leaped off their horses while it was still in motion, landing in a tumbled, delirious heap on the confetti-strewed grass. The other customers were clambering down now. Martin was the last to leave. He waited for complete absence of motion, as if to move earlier would be an impoliteness. Then he dismounted solemnly and came straight toward us, the balloon still clutched in his hand.

He didn't see us at first. And then his gaze fixed on Iris and his face shone with the joy of seeing her.

He ran to us. He took both of Iris's hands. He twisted the string of the yellow balloon around her finger, making it her balloon.

"Hello, Iris." He turned to me with his grave prefect's courtesy. "Hello, Peter."

I was amazed at his insensitivity. He was holding Iris's hands and yet he did not seem to notice that anything was wrong.

I said, "I thought you were in Acapulco, Martin."

"I was." He pushed back the unmanageable lock of hair. "I just drove up to——"

". . . to come to the fiesta," broke in Iris. "You love the fiesta, don't you, Martin? Every year you come to

81

the Santa Prisca fiesta." It was pitiful, her attempt to warn him.

He blinked and said confusedly, "Yes, the fiesta." And then, uncertainly, "What are you doing here, Iris?"

"She came to see Sally," I said.

"Oh, Sally." He seemed to lose interest. He stared down at his bronzed hands. I looked at them too. I noticed a white patch on the second finger of his right hand, where the sun had not touched the skin. It was pathetically obvious now.

I brought out of my pocket the ring that had dropped from Iris's finger in Sally's house.

"Your ring, Martin?"

He looked mildly puzzled. "Where on earth did you find it?"

I was going to answer, but Iris swung round on me, the yellow balloon bobbing on its string. Her eyes were blazing with hatred.

"A filthy, low-down trick."

Martin said, "What's the matter, Iris?"

"He's tricked you. The ring was at Sally's. I—I didn't know he got it. He's tricked you into admitting you were at Sally's. And Sally's dead."

In spite of the shock of knowing my wife could hate me, I felt a sense of relief. Was this then all it had been, the terror in Iris that had made her faint? Had it just been that she had found Martin's ring there and was terrified of what *he* might have done to Sally? Just Martin now? Not Iris?

I watched Martin's face absorbing what Iris had said. The change was a complex of so many emotions that it almost gave the impression of stupidity.

"Dead? Sally dead?"

"Yes, yes." Iris turned on me again. "Go away, Peter. Leave us alone."

"But——"

"Leave us alone. Can't you leave us alone?"

The steam organ was playing again, a sweet, halting tango. Iris's eyes bored into me, willing me out of existence, willing the destruction of everything except Martin.

I felt beaten, whipped. I said, "I'll go to Paco's. Look for Marietta. Join me later."

CHAPTER TWELVE

I left them. I didn't look back, but I could see them in my mind, standing there close together, oblivious to the thronging merrymakers. Martin slight, golden, to be protected, always to be protected, and Iris . . .

As I pushed my way through clusters of children, women with babies slung in shawls at their breasts, and soft-stepping Indians, a wave of excitement swept over the square. People at the far end, near the cathedral, started shouting and then a man darted into the Zocalo from a dark side street. On his shoulders he carried a big, brashly coloured effigy of a bull, bedecked with a scaffolding of fireworks. Already the fuse was sputtering gold in the darkness. I remembered that the fiesta of Santa Prisca always climaxed with a fireworks bull, and some of the mass excitement infected me.

The man was alone now in the centre of a jostling circle. With a quick flare, the first layer of fireworks ignited. Squibs banged. Red, blue, and yellow stars soared into the air and with them a rain of silver. Wildly bucking like a mock bull, the man charged the crowd, which scattered before him, shouting, screaming, laughing. The stars, the hissing, snapping squibs, exploded around them.

In the weird multicoloured light, the red cardboard bull on the man's shoulders reminded me of the bullfight, of Sally's jumping up, clapping her little hands, staring bright-eyed.

Blood and the ballet, Peter. Dressed up for death. That's the only thing that excites them, isn't it? Death.

The second layer of fireworks blazed with an even greater sparkle and hubbub. The square was afire with the thrill of it. And I thought, *This isn't death.*

Sally was death with her deep, dead malice, Iris is death with her love like a disease. And Marietta?

I wanted to see Marietta. I hurried into a side street, past the dimly glowing door of a pulque dive, headed toward the entrance to Paco's.

You have to go upstairs to Paco's. Drinks are served on a balcony looking down on the Zocalo. It has a certain shabby pretence to elegance. That's why the tourists go there. I climbed to the tiny hallway. Crowded in the entrance, a marimba and two violins were playing loudly, competing with the organ below. The noise was deafening.

A scattering of people stood at the inside bar. A few American women in the wrong clothes, schoolteachers probably, were giggling through their idea of the rumba with venal Mexican boys. Other people, Mexican and tourist, were strewed around at tables. French windows stood open, leading to the balcony. I looked around for Marietta's dark, secret head.

She wasn't there. I went to the French windows and stepped out on to the terrace. Down in the square, the bull was still on the rampage. The squeals and cries and the organ drowned out the marimba. Sparks and tinsel streamers of light flared up to me.

I saw Marietta at once. She was at a corner table alone, a tequila in front of her. Her face quivered in and out of brightness as the strange red, yellow, green lights of the fireworks followed each other. She wasn't looking down into the square. She was in profile to me, gazing out across the red-tiled roofs.

"Marietta."

She moved her head. The dark hair fell loosely around her face. She wore a green blouse with a white skirt, elegant with a touch of faded glamour, like something from Antibes in the twenties. The green blouse made the dark, unfathomable eyes green as laurel leaves. She looked up at me, calm, abstracted, not smiling and yet intimate.

"Hello, Peter," she said. "I hope you've got a cigarette. I'm too lazy to go to the bar for some."

I sat down next to her, facing the glow and dazzle of the Zocalo. I handed a cigarette to her and lit a match as her dark head came toward me. My hand was unsteady. I felt like a kid with his first love. But it was fear really, fear for what she might have done or what she might be accused of having done.

I said, "Why on earth did you come here, Marietta?"

She glanced up over the thin trickle of smoke from the cigarette. "I came to see Sally."

"I know. But why? What did you think you could do? Why didn't you tell me?"

"I thought it'd be better coming without you. I made Jake drive me down."

"Jake," I said. "Jake who you came screaming from last night."

The vague eyes watched me. "He has a car. I didn't want to come by bus. I didn't take him to Sally's. I left him here. I don't know what's happened to him."

Was that how she thought of me, I wondered? Jake who has a car. Peter who has a couch to sleep on.

Keeping my hands quiet on the table, I said, "And Sally? How was she?"

"Sally?" She shrugged. "The same."

"She didn't say anything?"

"Of course she said things. Sally always says things. She had a fine time."

"Doing what?"

"Oh, a spite fest. Little nasty threats and hints. Enjoying having me in her power. She's that unbelievable a woman, Peter. She talks about having people in her power. Like the pictures."

I saw the scene so clearly. Sally taunting Marietta with the hold she had over her, relishing it, not letting her know that she wasn't going to the police after all. *Making her squirm.*

"I shouldn't have gone," she was saying. "I only made things worse." Her eyes met mine again, perfectly at ease. I tried to penetrate their impenetrability. Could anyone put on so good an act, if . . . ?

I said, "And you left her? Sally?"

"What do you think I did—move in with her?"

"I mean, she was all right when you left her?"

"Of course." She picked up her tequila. "Why?"

"Because now," I said, "she's dead."

Marietta dropped her tequila. The little glass clattered across the table, coming to rest on its side against the central vase of magenta stock. I'd never seen her face like that before. The green eyes came alive with a leaping emotion that had fear in it and a strange, meaningless exaltation too. It was the least expected reaction.

Then I realized that she wasn't looking at me. She was staring at something over my shoulder. And I knew then that the glow, the new, half-fearful warmth that had thawed her, had nothing to do with what I had said. I doubt if she had even heard me. I turned to follow the direction of her rapt eyes.

Martin had come on to the terrace with Iris at his side.

They joined us at the table. Iris looked white and spent. Martin had her arm tucked into his. In his other hand he held the balloon.

I don't think he had noticed Marietta. She was just a girl sitting with me. He pulled two chairs together and sat down, still holding Iris's arm. Once again I was amazed by his absence of sensitivity. The tension in Marietta was so strong I could feel it like the throb of dance music very far away.

And then I remembered that they had quarrelled. Sally had deviously engineered a break. They hadn't seen each other or spoken to each other for years. Maybe he was deliberately ignoring her.

But I was wrong about that too. For he looked away from Iris across the table and saw Marietta. She was in control again. They looked at each other, grave, polite, as if they were people who had met once a long time ago at a house party. Friendly but completely casual. It was such an English meeting that it scarcely seemed real to me. Two people from another planet meeting the way people don't meet on earth.

"Hello, Marietta," he said.

"Hello, Martin."

And that was all. Martin turned back to Iris. Marietta lit a cigarette. Her hand wasn't even trembling.

"I'd better have another tequila, Peter. I spilt mine."

I called the waiter. He brought drinks for everyone. I said to Marietta, "You heard what I said about Sally?"

"Yes."

"You didn't know?"

"No, I didn't know." She picked a blossom from the magenta stock and started gravely to dissect it. "How did she die?"

"She fell off the balcony."

For a moment I thought she would be as fantastically stage-British as to say, "Oh." But she didn't say anything. Silence descended on the table, a silence charged by Iris's fear, my anxiety—and nothing from the Havens.

Suddenly Marietta said, "You came up from Acapulco, Martin?"

"Yes, Marietta."

She was peering at the stock blossom as if she wanted to examine the minutest detail of its botanical make-up. "To see Sally?"

The question hung in the air. Down in the Zocalo the pipe organ had stopped. We could hear the Paco orchestra now, the sob of the violins and the tinkle of the marimba.

I didn't pay much attention to what they were playing until I noticed a change in Martin. He had dropped Iris's arm. He was watching Marietta across the table. She wasn't looking at him. Then suddenly she was. I shall never forget her face, radiant, tentative.

The preposterously important question was still left unanswered. But they both rose. Martin released the yellow balloon. It floated up to the unpainted rafter. Martin went around the table and caught Marietta's waist. They drifted together, dancing, through the narrow, empty tables.

I listened to the music then, and I recognized the bittersweet, defeated melody.

> *Borrachitá, me voy par olvidarle.*
> *Le quero mucho y el también me quere.*
> *Borrachitá, me voy hasta la capital . . .*

It was the song the *mariachi* had played for Marietta last night at the Delta, the song that had brought the show, quiet tears to her eyes. I remembered a snatch of the dialogue.

"Someone was all for me once."

"Who?"

"Martin."

They swayed, very close together, Marietta's dark profile against Martin's golden cheek. And for the first time I resented them both, resented a glamour that seemed fake, a beauty that seemed false. Real people don't dance when they've just been told that a woman is dead, they seemed suddenly self-conscious to me, flotsam of charm, pallid ghosts unexorcised from an old novel by Michael Arlen.

> *Borrachitá, me voy hasta la capital*
> *Par servirme al patron*
> *Que me mandó llamar . . .*

They weren't dancing like brother and sister. They were dancing like lovers.

I looked at Iris. She was staring at them as if she had lost something secret and priceless.

CHAPTER THIRTEEN

While Martin and Marietta were dancing, I thought of Jake up at the Casa Haven, taking care of the body, taking care of the police, doing everything that Martin as Sally's husband should have been doing. I was beginning to see that was typical of the Havens. Whatever happened to them, there would always be someone else to do the dirty work.

I watched them moving, rapt, through the empty tables. I said to Iris, "I thought they had quarrelled."

"They never really quarrelled." Her voice was small, without body. "It was just Sally. Sally put ideas in Martin's head, kept them apart."

"Now Sally's dead and they're celebrating. What could be more reasonable?"

My wife turned to me with her old ferocity. "You don't understand Martin. No one understands him."

"Except you?"

"He isn't like other people. Martin's half genius, half——"

". . . louse?"

She said gratingly, "If you have to be that spiteful, it's hopeless between us."

I was watching Marietta. Compared with her, Iris seemed pale, almost insignificant to me. Already the rope that I had thought would keep me forever hog-tied to Iris was fraying. Another strand had snapped. I could even visualize a time in the future when she would mean no more to me than "the wind goin' over my hand." It hurt losing something, even though it was a thing I was better off without.

I knew someone had to come out into the open sometime. I said, "Did you kill Sally? Or are you scared that Martin did?"

She sat very still, not saying anything.

"You knew Martin had been there," I said. "The whole thing with the ring was pitiful. Was it something you arranged together, you and Martin? Iris, what happened?"

She seemed to have grown smaller, but she still did not speak. The silver tinkle of the marimba rattled from the inside bar. Marietta and Martin were still dancing.

I went on. "You've got to tell me. There's only Jake between you—and God knows what. You can't rely on Jake. You don't even know what his game is. Don't be like Martin, drifting along being a pilgrim, expecting everything to fix itself. Hate me if you like. God knows I'm getting used to it. But tell me the truth."

She said icily, "Jake was there. He said it was an accident. The police say it was an accident."

I saw it was useless. She thought of me too much as an enemy. I felt terribly sorry for her. I said, "The head's pretty deep in the gas oven, isn't it?"

She was suddenly pleading. "You don't suppose I'm happy, do you?"

I didn't rise to the plea. "I don't know what you are any more. And I don't know what you've done. But I do know we've got to get rooms for to-night. I'll call the Borda. How about you and Martin? Separate rooms?"

She looked as if I'd slapped her. "Of course."

"All this—and separate rooms. A fine romance."

There was a rich, tourist luxury about the Hotel de la Borda. It was a relief to be in a normal atmosphere where people were doing normal things, sitting in deep chairs, reading the *Readers' Digest*, and discussing to-morrow's sight-seeing trip. The management was polite about our absence of luggage. We were taken up to beautiful, clean rooms with bright modern Mexican furniture and staggering views of the terraced town.

Jake, who appeared shortly after us with the news that everything was in control until the inquest to-morrow, vetoed any further discussion that night, although, heaven knows, the others showed no signs of wanting to discuss anything ever. We broke up and went to our separate rooms. I slumped into a yellow tape chair by the open window and lit a cigarette. Then I called downstairs for a drink. When it came, I stared out at the dying lights of the town, watching them vanish one after the other as fiesta-tired Mexicans dropped on to their rush sleeping mats.

I thought about Sally. A few hours ago she had been so powerful; she had had three lives to play with and she had been enjoying herself to the hilt. Now she was dead, brushed away like a dead fly by a cryptic Californian and a Mexican policeman whose uncle was a carpenter. Something had happened on that balcony. What? With whom? Marietta's face, Martin's face, Iris's face rose in my mind. I started to worry; then I thought, "Why the hell should I worry? What's it to me?"

I finished my drink.

There was a knock on the door. I said, "Come in." It was Martin Haven. He had taken off his jacket and tie. The sun-silvered blond hair was tousled. He was carrying a bottle of some kind of capsules.

He smiled his sudden, trusting smile that made you feel you'd be a heel if you didn't love him more than anyone in the world.

"Hope I'm not bothering you, Peter."

"Of course not."

"There's no drinking water in my room. You can't drink water out of the taps in this country. I thought you had some perhaps."

There were a pitcher and glasses on a side table. I nodded to them. He splashed some water in a glass, took two capsules out of the bottle, and swallowed them.

"Thank you."

"What you taking?"

"Just sleeping tablets. I can't sleep in Mexico." He crossed to the bed and sat down on it, tucking his legs under him. He watched me. The blue eyes were utterly guileless.

He said, "Something I ought to tell you, Peter."

"There is?"

"Yes." He paused. "I was at Sally's to-night."

"I know you were."

"I know you do." The smile came unexpectedly. "That's why I'm telling you."

91

I waited.

"She called me yesterday in Acapulco, asked me to come, told me not to say anything about it to Iris."

How many times had I heard a version of that story?

"And when you arrived, she was alive?"

"Naturally."

"What happened?"

"She was quite decent, really. Said everything might be arranged."

"No quarrel?"

"No, nothing of that sort."

"And yet your ring was left behind. What happened? Just slip off?"

"Oh, no. She asked for it. She'd given it to me when we were married. She wanted it as a keepsake." He looked at me gravely. "She loved me, you know."

"Seems it's quite an epidemic."

He didn't rise to that. He slid a leg out from under him and gripped his sun-gold ankle. "Funny. Everything's violently changed, isn't it?"

"Violently."

"That end of the balcony was always rotten. In the rainy season the rain washed down that way off the porch roof. There's no gutter."

"There isn't?"

"Peter." He hesitated. "The police—they won't think anything odd, will they?"

"Depends on what you mean by odd."

"I mean, Sally being dead with the situation . . ."

I said, "What did Sally have on you and Marietta?"

I could see the blood coursing up behind the smooth boy's skin of his face. "How do you know about that?"

"Sally was at my place in Mexico last night. She said she had enough proof to throw you both in jail. What was it?"

He said stiffly, "I don't see what that has to do with anything. It was just a—personal matter."

"I'm not being vulgarly curious. You asked me if the police will think anything odd. If they find evidence that she could have had you and Marietta in jail, they'll think things are plenty odd. Did she have proof? Sally?"

The flush was still there. "Yes. I believe she did."

"Where'd she keep it?"

"I don't know."

Impulsively he got off the bed and dropped to the floor at my feet, squatting with his arms resting on his crossed legs. It seemed almost impossible that he was a grown man. He was like a little English boy trying to cozen a half-crown out of Pater.

"You won't say anything about this to the police, Peter?"

"I won't say anything to anyone. I don't speak Spanish. You'll have to square Jake."

"Jake? He doesn't know, does he?"

"I don't know what Jake knows and what he doesn't."

He said, "Who is he, anyway?"

"I don't know."

He said with sudden, savage bitterness, "Marietta knows. Or perhaps she doesn't. You don't know much about people who pick you up in bars."

"This isn't the time to sit in moral judgment on Marietta."

He seemed to forget Marietta. His face lightened.

"There's something I've been meaning to ask you. You're not angry with me, are you?"

"About what?"

"About Iris?"

He was genuinely worried. I could tell that. Martin couldn't bear to have anyone not liking him. He'd stolen my wife. But that wasn't anything. I still had to be his friend, take him out to tea with plenty of crumpets and cucumber sandwiches. What could you do with your wife's lover when he was this way? Pat him on the head and say, "Okay, Junior. Run along now. It's way past your bedtime?"

He said gravely, "It couldn't be helped, you know, Peter. Things like that can't be helped."

"You should put that in a book."

He was so slight and yet so closely knit. He made me feel big and clumsy. "Most people don't understand, Peter. Because I know what I want and get what I want, they think I'm heartless. I'm not. If you've got to live, you can only live the way you want with the things you want."

"If you can get them."

He looked faintly puzzled. Perhaps it had just crept into his consciousness that some people couldn't always get what they wanted.

"Right now I need Iris," he said.

He needed Iris right now. We were all supposed to cluster around and clap our hands.

He got up and picked the bottle of sleeping capsules off the green-and-white bedspread. He yawned and then grinned.

"The pills are beginning to work. Better get to bed."

"Do you carry that stuff around with you all the time? Even when you expect to be home before nightfall?"

"Oh, no. Sally gave me these. I'd left them at the house. She knows I need them horribly."

Nothing had been resolved, but he seemed to think it had. He held out his hand. There was nothing to do but play it his way. I took the hand. It was warm and dry and the nails were almost silver against the sun-tanned skin.

"You're being an awful sport, Peter."

"Think nothing of it," I said. "It isn't cricket not helping a pilgrim."

"Pilgrim? What do you mean?"

"Nothing," I said. "Skip it."

He left. I wondered if a husband-lover relationship had ever developed this way before. It probably had. Everything had happened before. I wished I had another drink, but I couldn't be bothered to pick up the phone and order one. I thought of Sally's evidence against Martin and Marietta lying, heaven knew where, for the police to find. Then I thought of another thing. I thought of the sheet of paper which Jake had pulled out of Sally's typewriter. I knew then that I wouldn't sleep unless I found out what it was. I left my room and went down the corridor to Jake's. I knocked.

He called, "Who is it?"

"Peter."

"Come in, Peter."

He was sitting on the bed, stripped to the waist, taking off his shoes. He had the torso of a champion boxer. In perfect trim too. No thickening around the hips. He grinned at me over his shoulder. There was a pint of whiskey on the table beside him.

"Well, well," he said. "What can I do for you?"

"You can give me a drink for one thing."

"Sure, sure."

He poured a stiff shot for me and patted the bed next to him. I took the drink and sat down. He kicked off his shoes and started pulling off his socks. He wasn't helping me.

I said, "What did you take out of Sally's typewriter? A letter?"

"Sally's typewriter?" He twisted around, giving me the naïve blue stare. "Oh, that."

"Yeah," I said. "That."

He shrugged and the muscles rippled under the white skin. "That wasn't anything, Peter."

"Then why did you take it?"

He grinned. "Sloppy, leaving things in typewriters. I hate sloppiness."

I said, "For the second time, why are you doing all this?"

He twisted around on the bed. He put his heavy bare arm on my shoulder. I smelled sweat, not subway sweat, gymnasium sweat. I wished he wouldn't be so affectionate, or, if he had to be affectionate, that the obscure, sinister undertone wasn't there.

"Listen, you want that accident to stay nice and tidy, don't you?"

"Of course."

"You want that inquest to pan out all right tomorrow?"

I nodded.

"Okay, I'm fixing it, aren't I?"

"It seems so."

"Then take a load off your mind. Quit worrying. Relax."

I said, "I'm not likely to relax until I know who you are and what you're doing this for."

He got up and stripped off his pants. He glanced at me over his shoulder, making a mock clucking sound.

"There you go again. There isn't no satisfying some guys."

95

He shook the pants, folded them neatly, and put them on a chair. He came back to the bed and nudged me with his elbow.

"Hey, get off of there. Jake's going to bye-bye."

I got up. He pulled back the sheets and flopped into the bed with a grunt of satisfaction.

"Light me a cigarette, Peter. Lazy. That's me."

I lit a cigarette and stuck it between his lips. A big arm came up from under the sheets and took it. He was watching me.

"We'll get along, Peter, if you play it my way."

I didn't know what he meant, of course.

"And one thing you'd better learn is to stop asking questions when Uncle Jake isn't giving the answers."

He pushed himself up. The bedclothes dropped away from him.

"There's one thing we'd better get straight, though—plenty quick."

"What?"

"Which of those dames are you after—Iris or Marietta?"

The question caught me off balance. Which was I after, anyway? Under the cropped red hair, his blue eyes were blatantly intimate, as if we were two men trading hot telephone numbers.

I said, "Maybe that's a question Uncle Peter isn't answering."

"Okay. If that's your attitude. Okay." He puffed cigarette smoke, curling his lips so that they looked almost negroid. "But get one thing straight, baby. I'm making a play for Marietta. That kid does things to me. I want her."

A fleeting image came of Marietta last night, Marietta with her hands cold as ice, Marietta shivering.

"Yeah." His stare was still on me like a challenge. "I want her. And when Jake wants something, he gets it. See what I mean?"

"Yes," I said. "I see what you mean."

"Then there's not going to be any sloppiness about that." He twisted around in bed, crushed the cigarette into a tray, and turned out the bedside lamp.

"Now, scram, Peter. If there's one thing I don't like in a bedroom with the lights out, it's a man."

I went out of the room. Marietta's room was next door. I tapped lightly. I tried the handle. The room wasn't locked. I pushed open the door.

She was standing fully dressed with her back to me, combing her dark hair and looking out into the moonlight. She hadn't heard my knock. Then, suddenly conscious of a presence, she turned.

It was the same each time I saw her. Her beauty caught my breath as if I was seeing her for the first time. She was straight and slim as a sapling. Her eyes were green like leaves.

I said, "I just came with a little practical advice. Keep your door locked."

"Wasn't it locked?"

"It wasn't. And it better be."

"Why?"

"Unless you want Jake to get chummy with you."

"Jake!"

"Marietta, you weren't born yesterday." I went to her and put my hands on her arms. "Or were you?"

Her face was very close to mine. I saw her eyes change as if a sprinkle of frost had come. She was stiff, unyielding.

"Now, baby," I said, "no shivering."

Suddenly she melted in my arms. "Stay with me," she said. "Stay with me, Peter. Just for to-night."

I ran my hand down her dark, soft hair.

"Please. Peter . . ."

She was shivering now, and she was gripping me to her as if I was the only thing that could warm her.

I said, "Marietta, tell me something. It's time now. What do you want? Who do you want?"

"How do I know? Does anyone know?"

"Martin knows what he wants," I said.

She reacted to the name like a dog reacting to a whip. She clung to me. Her lips moved over my cheek, and she whispered with an abandon that was more like despair than passion. "Stay with me, Peter. Stay with me. Stay with me."

97

CHAPTER FOURTEEN

The inquest was, to me, astonishingly uneventful. It was held next morning in Sally's sun-splashed living-room. Nothing had been changed. The tuberoses, yellowing slightly, still stood in their blue and white Oaxaca vase by the French windows. The furniture had not been altered to present a more official appearance. The man in charge, a heavy, middle-aged man with black, alert eyes, sat on the couch with a coffee table in front of him as a desk. A group of nondescript people, jurors or hangers-on, I was never sure which, stood respectfully at one end of the room. The Captain of Police and his two honey-coloured buddies sat squashed tightly and stiffly together on the long piano stool. Jake, Iris, Marietta, Martin, and I lounged in the gay Domus chairs.

Since no one else was sufficiently bilingual, Jake was chosen as interpreter. This to me seemed rash on the part of the law, but since they apparently had every confidence in him, and since there was absolutely no concrete evidence left to make the accident questionable, I suppose it was reasonable enough.

The Captain of Police and his two assistants testified first. Then Jake gave his own story in Spanish. Iris and I, through Jake, were called upon only to substantiate the "simplified" version of the discovery of the corpse. The three of us together, we said, had paid Sally a social visit and had found her dead. Martin and Marietta had been coached by Jake before breakfast. They gave evidence that they had visited Sally much earlier in the afternoon, had talked to her about unimportant family matters and had left her in good spirits. Owing to the fiesta, there was little risk that anyone had been observant enough to notice the time of their actual arrivals and departures from the Casa Haven. Martin was called again, and the carpenter uncle of the Captain of Police. They both supported each other as to the rottenness of the balcony. No mention was made of the repair visit which the uncle had failed to make. The absence of a gutter and the insidious effect of the rain were played up to the hilt.

After a lot of talking, some excited, some bored and plodding, the Coroner, or whatever he was, closed his notebook and stood up. The people in the corner had something to say about it all. Then we were dismissed.

Everyone in the room must have known about the situation between Martin, Sally, and Iris. But, so far as I could tell, it wasn't broached. But then the Mexicans are a polite race and, from their experience of the United States citizens resident there, divorce and sex intrigue were as natural a part of American life as burros and tortillas were for the Mexican peasant.

In spite of my own personal misgivings, the inquest had been far from a mockery of justice. The house had been thoroughly searched. Obviously Sally's claimed "proof" of a past misdeed committed by Martin and Marietta had not been found. Thanks to Jake, there was nothing else to find. Things might well have worked out the same way in Westchester County, unless some sensation-smelling journalist had pushed an investigation for its headline value.

After a great deal of handshaking and smiling with the Coroner, Jake expansively invited us all for a drink at Paco's, which was very post-fiesta. A couple of dark, languid waiters coped with a group of bouncing American schoolteachers plastered with Taxco silver jewellery. Below the terrace in the Zocalo, pigs grunted their way through the tumbled confetti and streamers. The carrousel was dead. A small, solemn boy was swinging himself in the pink swing. Flies swarmed over the stalls of candied fruit. Up between the feathery twin steeples, the Star of Bethlehem had reverted to being a grimy cardboard cut-out.

At the head of the table, Jake grinned and lifted his tequila Collins. *"Salud,"* he said.

His bright eyes moved from one of us to the other. "Well, babies, there may be quite a cackle of gossip among the Americans, but gossip doesn't signify. You'll have to come down and weep at the funeral, I guess. But after that I figure you can consider that little episode closed."

"Thanks to you," I said.

"Yeah, buddy, you've said it." He looked right at me without smiling. "Thanks to me."

He turned to Martin. "You'd better go to Mexico City and start talking to Sally's lawyer about the property. Know his address?"

Martin looked uncomfortable, as if he weren't accustomed to people mentioning such worldly subjects. "Yes," he said. "I think so."

"You inherit everything, don't you?"

"I believe I do," said Martin.

"Okay. Start plaguing the lawyer. The sooner the better." Jake took a gulp of his drink. "That's what people are going to expect you to do. Better not disappoint them."

I don't think Martin got the crack.

"Of course," Jake went on, "it'll take a little time to get things smoothed out, but I can't see as there'll be any trouble."

He swallowed his drink abruptly and summoned the waiter to pay the check. When it was paid, he got up. The morning sunlight played on the red, cropped hair. He looked like a good-natured, rather dumb wrestler, the clean kid from the Y.M.C.A. who had the crowd rooting for him.

"Well, it's been swell knowing you folks," he said. "Guess there's nothing more I can do for you right now, so I'll be on my way."

Marietta, sitting next to me, stiffened. I felt pretty surprised myself.

"You're going?" said Iris.

"Sure." The white teeth flashed. "I've always wanted to make Acapulco. The playground of the world. Guess I could do with a little sun-baking for a while. Sun fiend, that's Jake."

He moved to the terrace and gazed down at the suspended gaiety of the Zocalo.

"Not as big a drop as the drop from Sally's balcony," he murmured thoughtfully.

Iris slipped her hand into Martin's. There was an uncomfortable silence.

Jake turned again, grinning. "Maybe I'll give you a buzz when I get back to Mexico, just in case any other of your pals falls off of anything. How's about an address?"

Iris looked at Martin. "We don't know where we'll be yet. But you can always get us all through Peter."

I scribbled my telephone number on a card and handed it to him. He pushed it into his pants pocket without reading it.

"Okay, kids. This is it."

Iris suddenly said, "Thanks so much, Jake. You've been wonderful."

He grinned. "Think nothing of it. Got to help your pals, haven't you? Nothing to it, anyway. Just a spot of simplification."

He moved to Marietta and watched her with flagrantly masculine interest. A faint smile played around his lips. He put his big hands on her shoulders and kissed her full on the mouth.

"Sorry about this, baby. You don't mind having me walk out on you? Peter can drive you home, can't he?"

Marietta's green eyes watched him. "Yes, Jake, Peter can drive me home."

That had me staggered. I had been certain this was the moment he had chosen to drop his role of disinterested pal and come out in his true colours, whatever they were. But here he was walking out of our lives. And even bequeathing me Marietta too.

He shook my hand. He shook Iris's hand. He slapped Martin on the back.

"Well, kids, take care of yourselves."

He waved and strolled away toward the inner bar. As he disappeared, he started to whistle softly under his breath.

The tune he was whistling was "I'll Be Seeing You."

I was sure then that we would be seeing him—soon. That was when the trouble would begin.

CHAPTER FIFTEEN

I drove Marietta home. She was abstracted, almost un-friendly. As soon as we reached Mexico City, she left me. She got out of the car by the Caballito and walked away, slim and straight, through the clear sunlight toward the Arch of the Revolution. That night Iris telephoned and told me that Martin had moved into the apartment of a friend who was out of town. She had taken a room at the Guardiola. At least they had enough sense for that.

After the phone call, all three of them slipped out of my life as suddenly and completely as Jake and Sally Haven.

I read in the paper that Martin and Marietta had at-tended Sally's funeral in Taxco. It was a small, uninter-ested paragraph. That was all. If my memory of Jake had not been so vivid, I could have pretended that the whole Sally episode was over.

I expected Marietta to call, but she didn't. Something, pride maybe, kept me from calling her. Then after a couple of days of loneliness I telephoned her number to be told that she didn't live there any more. They didn't know where she was.

I picked up Martin's novel in a little bookstore on Hildago. Apart from Iris's unqualified superlatives, I had been told nothing about it. I started to read it sceptically, but after the first few pages I was absorbed. Martin's talent was authentic.

The story was simple. It was about a brother and sister growing up in an English country house. They lived in a world of their own, bound together by a love that was inarticulate but poignantly constant. They thought life would go on forever the same, with the wonder of catching black and yellow newts in the cress-filled ponds, the perilous climbing of elm trees after rooks' eggs, the greedy scramble for blackberries on the dusty August lanes. Then, gradually, they began to find out that nothing lasts. They grew a little older and became adolescently awkward with each other. They tried to make things stay the way that they had been. But they were inevitably defeated. The boy was finally sent off to public school, and the book ended heartbreakingly with his return for the summer holidays. He brought with him a new school friend whom he worshipped. They shared the same bedroom. They were inseparable. He was lost in a new love and the girl was forgotten.

It was obviously a picture of Martin and Marietta. Even the cowslip hill was there, the hawthorn staffs, the nightgowns, the pilgrims. It was written with a gentle tenderness that gave me a new respect for Martin. But mostly I was haunted by the portrait of Marietta as the little girl with the green, green eyes, the flying dark pigtails, the dirty knees, and the great, tragic love in her heart.

After I had read the book, she was seldom out of my mind. I started to frequent the bars we used to patronize. I never saw her. Gradually she became almost an obsession. I would think I saw her dark head in the blue light that bathed the dancing couples at Ciro's. When the peeling swing doors of the Cantina Delta were pushed open, I turned to look, sure it would be she. But it wasn't.

The thought grew insidiously that she was with Jake, that they had made some secret arrangement, that they were together in Acapulco. I had visions of them on some lonely silver beach at Los Hornos, Jake big as an ox in swimming trunks, Marietta's clean, firm body giving itself voluptuously to the sun.

One evening Iris called. Her voice sounded constrained, awkward.

"Hello, Peter."

"Hello."

There was a silence. I said, "How's Martin coming along with the lawyer?"

"Everything seems to be going swimmingly. The will's

very uncomplicated. Everything to Martin. The lawyer says it's just a question of getting it probated or something."

"Fine."

"Sally was an orphan, you know. There aren't any near relatives to contest."

"Finer." I asked, "Has it occurred to Martin to refuse the money?"

"Why on earth should he do that?"

"Under the circumstances, do you imagine Sally would have wanted him to have it?"

"Really, Peter, that's awfully rarefied, isn't it? After all, he put up with her all those years. You can't expect him to let the money go to waste. Someone has to have it."

"Sure," I said.

She seemed genuinely puzzled, and I might have expected it. Ethical niceties don't mean much to the feminine mind. Particularly not to the feminine mind in love. Probably she had already managed to convince herself that there had been nothing out of the ordinary about Sally's death.

I had guessed what she was having such difficulty in trying to say. I helped her. "With the money coming through soon, I guess you'll be thinking about marriage. Want me to get the divorce wheels working?"

"Peter, it's awful, but would you? That's what I called about. Do you mind terribly?"

A few weeks ago I had minded terribly. Did I care now?

"You can put all the blame on me."

"Don't worry about that. I'll find out what to do tomorrow."

"I'm awfully sorry."

"Don't be."

The silence came again, but she still stayed on the wire.

I said, "And how's Martin?"

"Oh, he's fine." She added rather quickly, "Of course, I don't see a great deal of him. He thinks it's wiser that way right now."

"And Marietta?"

"Marietta? Don't you know?"

"I don't know anything."

"She's living with Martin."

"She is?"

"Yes, the apartment's big enough for two. She moved in last week."

I had been imagining Marietta with Jake. I saw now how shoddy a thought it had been. I should have known it was Martin. A blight seemed to descend. Absurdly, I found myself wishing that I had been right, that it had been Jake.

"Yes," said Iris, "she's being perfectly wonderful. She cooks for him, does everything."

"She does?"

"She even helps with the new book. Every night they're together, talking about—about old times, remembering things from the past, the governess from Scotland with the elastic-sided boots, whether it was apricot jam or strawberry jam they liked best with their muffins, whether it was five or six eggs in the double-breasted lapwings' nest back of the third gardener's cottage." She laughed. "So English. So veddy, veddy English."

I wished she hadn't laughed. It hurts to have someone you've loved very much giving herself away like that.

Pity for her rose in me almost like physical desire. I wanted to say something to comfort her, to assure her, uselessly, that you didn't get jealous of a man's sister.

"All the time," she said into the phone. "She never leaves him. That's why I see him so seldom. All the time they're together there in the apartment—remembering."

Later, the Mexicana telephone rang again. I hurried to answer it, knowing it wouldn't be Marietta, but hoping. A familiar, bantering male voice said, "Hi, Peter. Guess who this is."

"Hello, Jake," I said with a sinking heart.

"How's tricks with you, Peter?"

"Okay."

"Just back from Acapulco yesterday. Boy, what a place, Acapulco. Boy, what a tan I got.

"Yeah. I intend to throw a little party to show it off.

Got quite a fancy suite at the Reforma. How's about coming over?"

"It's late," I said.

A cluck sounded over the wire. "Hey, Peter, what's got into you? Who ever heard of not going to a party because it's late?"

"All right," I said.

"That's more like it. How's about the others—Marietta, Iris, the widower? This has got to be a real reunion."

I said, "I don't know where Martin and Marietta are, but Iris is at the Guardiola."

"She knows where the others are at?"

"I guess so. Want me to call Iris?"

He laughed. "No, sir, I think they'd kind of appreciate it more if the old maestro called himself. Okay, Peter. Hop a taxi. Suite two seventeen."

"Right away?"

"Sure. The whisky's itching."

My car was parked outside. I drove up the stately night quietness of Insurgentes, turned into the Paseo de la Reforma, and parked outside the Reforma Hotel. I had a pretty good idea what was coming.

CHAPTER SIXTEEN

Jake's suite was indeed fancy. I wondered how much it set him back per day. I found him alone, in his shirt sleeves. He was fiddling around a dumb-waiter loaded with glasses and ice and whisky. His big forearms, thrusting out from the rolled sleeves, were red-brown from the sun.

He swung round, grinning at me cheerfully. He came over and banged me on the shoulder.

"Hiyah, Peter, old horse."

The red hair was even more closely cropped. His blue eyes watched me, bland, friendly.

"Get a load of the tan."

"Yes," I said.

He yanked his shirt out of his trousers and pulled it up, revealing a broad expanse of brown chest and stomach.

"The real McCoy, Pete."

"You've been working hard."

"Sure. Want me to take off my pants too?"

"I get the general idea with the pants on."

Leaving his unbuttoned shirt flopping outside his trousers, he crossed and poured two drinks. He handed me mine and lifted his glass.

"*Salud.*"

"*Salud.*"

"We can be boys together a couple of minutes, Pete. The others'll be right along."

"They're coming?"

The blue eyes opened wide. "Of course they're coming. I called Iris. She was charmed—absolutely charmed. She's bringing Martin and Marietta."

He sat on the arm of an overstuffed chair and propped the hand which held his drink on his knees.

"So Marietta's moved in with Martin," he said.

"Yes."

He gave me a knowing wink. "Smart, that babe. Cashing in quick, ain't she?"

I almost hated him then. "You don't imagine Martin's wallowing in Sally's money yet, do you? Those legal things take time."

He nodded soberly. "Sure. Guess they do. Still, she's playing it the right way, getting in on the ground floor."

The door buzzer rang. He jumped to answer it. The three of them came in, Martin between Marietta and Iris. Jake greeted them with a whoop of delight. He slapped Martin's back. He grinned at Iris. He picked Marietta up and swirled her around with her feet off the floor.

"Hi, Marietta. How's my girl?"

Martin looked like thunder, but said nothing. Jake put Marietta down. She gave him a fleeting smile.

"Hello, Jake."

She saw me and came straight to me. I was amazed at the change in her. I had never seen her so radiant. Her eyes weren't the lost-child eyes. The snow had melted. She was like a goddess of spring. I wondered whether she knew I'd been waiting in night after night for her to call.

"Hello, Peter. Martin's just finished work."

Jake came up behind her, with a drink in his hand. He slid his arm around her waist.

"Scotch, baby. I've got everything else, but we're drinking Scotch to-night. Scotch is a luxury in this country. Celebration."

She took the drink absently, as if he was just a man bringing a drink. She was still smiling at me.

"Peter, why don't you visit us sometimes? You're so exclusive."

Jake poured drinks for Martin and Iris.

"Sit down, sit down," he said. "Get a load off those pretty feet."

Martin and Iris sat down together on a couch. Marietta dropped on to the arm of my chair, balancing herself on my shoulder.

Jake stood in the middle of the room and lifted his glass.

"To our reunion," he said.

We politely lifted our glasses.

"Sure and you're a sight for sore eyes," he went on. "Couldn't get you all out of my mind. Know what? After you, the folks in Acapulco were colourless as cellophane."

He strolled across to the couch on which Martin and Iris were sitting. The lazy grace of his big body was ominous to me. He grinned down at Martin.

"How's things coming with the lawyer?"

Martin looked up at him, grave, polite, "They seem to be progressing."

"That's fine. That surely is fine. Quite a lot of dough coming to you, isn't there?"

Martin said, "I believe there is quite a lot, yes."

"How much?"

Martin's dark blue eyes watched him rather dazedly as it he couldn't believe his ears. "I . . . I think the lawyer said it was somewhere in the neighbourhood of two million dollars."

"Swell," said Jake. "Swell and dandy. How about writing me a cheque? Fifty thousand, maybe, to begin with?"

His voice hadn't lost its tone of amiable banter. I don't think the others grasped what he said. I did, of course, because I'd been expecting the worst for days.

Martin was still looking at him, puzzled. Then his vivid, golden smile came. "A joke. I'm sorry. I'm always slow on jokes."

Jake smiled back. "If it's too early right now, I can wait a couple of weeks. But only a couple of weeks. That's why I went to Acapulco. To give you time to get the ball rolling. Little breather. But after two weeks, I'll want action. If things haven't panned out by then, I don't imagine you with your prospects will have much trouble in raising the fifty thousand from a moneylender. I can put you on to a couple right here in town. Reliable, discreet, easy rates of interest."

Marietta's hand was gripping hard into my shoulder. Martin got up and sat down again. Iris looked as if she had heard the knell of doom. She had, of course.

To me it was almost a relief having him come out with it at last.

Iris said in a voice that was meant to be calm, "Just why should Martin give you fifty thousand dollars, Jake?"

"Yes," I said. "Why?"

He looked disappointed in me. "Now, Peter, we all want to keep this friendly, don't we? We don't want to wallow in ugly details."

I said, "Fifty thousand dollars is an ugly detail. If one, why not more?"

"Well, well." He sighed. "We live and learn." He crossed to a chair from which he could keep us all under observation. He sat down, hitching his pants up at the knees. "I'd have thought nice people like you'd have felt a decent gratitude. I'd have thought you'd have wanted me to have a cut—after all I did for you."

He was stripped for action now. The friendly rough-diamond act was over. The real Jake was as exposed as the big bare arms and patch of brown stomach visible behind the unbuttoned shirt. I had a pretty good idea what he was going to say.

"Well?" he said. "You want it?"

None of the others spoke. I saw that I, as usual, would have to take over. I didn't have much hope of success.

I said, "Okay, Jake. Give with the ugly details."

He was watching Marietta, the lids half lowered lazily over his eyes. She was pale now, cold and lonely as the snow on Ixtacihuatl.

He said, "Well, it's mostly about dames falling off of balconies. Where I come from, if a dame leans against a rotten balustrade and it gives way, the piece of balustrade hits the ground *before* she does, not *after*. Check?"

"Go on," I said.

"Then, where I come from too, a dame, taking a stroll out on to her own balcony, has to be powerful clumsy to lose a slipper and knock over a vase of flowers in transit. Check?"

"More," I said.

He grinned. "I'm only just beginning, Peter. There's this letter that was in her typewriter, for example. It's a funny kind of letter for a dame to be in the middle of writing when she happens accidentally to fall off of a balcony. Like me to read it?"

This was where the real danger started.

"Read it," I said.

He pulled a shabby wallet out of his pocket and made a great show of searching. "Where's it now? I could have sworn——Oh, sure. Here we are."

He produced a piece of paper. He unfolded it.

"Quite a letter," he said. "She was writing it to this Mr. Johnson, the lawyer guy here in Mexico. It says:

"DEAR MR. JOHNSON,—I've tried to call you all day but the connections are terrible. I'm writing because this is very very important. You've got to come immediately because I'm going to change my will. . . .

He looked up from the paper at Martin. "Hear that?"

Martin glared back at him. Martin could look tough too. He reminded me of a golden-glove kid facing up to the heavyweight champ.

"Go on," he said.

"Sure. Let me see now. Pretty sloppy typer, Sally. Guess she was het up. Here we are. . . .

"I'm cutting my husband out completely, I don't know where I'm going to leave my money and I don't care, just so Martin doesn't get any. He's run off with another woman and wants me to divorce him. I won't divorce him. But it's not just because he's run off that I want to change my will. It's because I'm afraid. Mr. Johnson, you've got to believe me. I'm not being hysterical. I'm afraid he'll murder me for the money, either he will or the woman will. And it's not only that. I know something about him and his sister, something that could put them in jail for years. They know that too. I'm afraid of them all, Mr. Johnson, desperately afraid. That's why I'm writing to . . ."

He stopped reading. "That's where she broke off to take a stroll on the balcony. Needed a little fresh air maybe." He folded the paper and put it neatly back in his wallet. "Someone was a dope not to notice that letter and destroy it."

He finished his drink and rose. "Anyone ready for a freshener?"

No one said anything. He poured himself another drink and half turned to glance at Martin.

"Now, Martin, I'm not saying you necessarily murdered Sally. Maybe Marietta did. Maybe Iris did. But you're all so palsy-walsy that I figure you'd like to stick together. And what's fifty thousand bucks to a guy who's dragging down two million smackers just because a little lady got so forgetful and fell off of her balcony before she could lick an envelope and a postage stamp?"

Martin's lips were pale. "That's all the evidence you've got?"

"It'll do, won't it?"

I said, "We get the idea. No fifty thousand dollars and you go to the police."

He grimaced. "Well, Peter, I guess I could, couldn't I, if I felt in an ornery mood?"

"You're forgetting something," I said. "You discovered the body. You suppressed the evidence. That makes you an accessory after the fact."

"Peter, I'm surprised at you." He grinned. "No, on second thought, I'm not. You don't know the whole story about me. I figured it'd simplify things to be kind of reticent for a while. You see, I'm a private detective. A private dick to you. Like to see the credentials? Pretty."

He fumbled some papers out of his pocket and tossed them to me. They proclaimed that Jacob Lord, whose photograph was affixed thereunto, was a licensed private investigator in the State of California. That's what he looked like, of course. Now I knew, it was written all over him.

"Yeah, Peter," he said. "Sally hired me, imported me from California a couple of days before she died. She was scared of being murdered by Martin or Marietta or Iris, she said. My job was to keep an eye on all of you and protect her. That's why I picked Marietta up at the bar."

He grinned. "Swell job I did of protecting, didn't I? But that's not the point. The point is the police'll feel

112

kind of sorry for me, losing a valuable client like that. And, of course, they'll understand why I held up the evidence temporarily. After all, I was in your confidence. It was a perfect set-up for a little preliminary investigation. I'll say I needed an accident verdict at the inquest to put you all off your guard."

I said, "And you think they'll believe you?"

"Natch, Pete, old pal."

"The police aren't crazy for private dicks."

"That's where you're wrong, baby. Here in Mexico, a private investigator from the States—he's a big shot. Besides, that whole set-up in Taxco's ready to break. It didn't break just because I handled it fine. But they all know the Martin-Iris-Sally set-up. There's the will, too, Martin inheriting. The moment murder's mentioned, even with a tenth of the evidence I got . . ." He shrugged expressively.

"It'll only be your word against ours." I sounded more arrogant than I felt. "I'll swear the balustrade wasn't over Sally's legs. Iris and I will swear there was no slipper, no over-turned vase, nothing in the typewriter. After all, that letter you just read us isn't signed. You could have typed it yourself. We will say you framed the whole thing."

"For why?"

"For fifty thousand dollars."

"And you think they'll believe you?" He was mocking me by quoting my own words back.

"Why not? I'm as disinterested a party as you."

He looked at Iris. He looked at Marietta. He winked at me. "Disinterested, eh?" He paused. "No, Pete, I'm kind of afraid they wouldn't go for that. You see, there *was* a slipper, there *was* an overturned vase, there *was* a letter in the typewriter. Remember? Of course, if your memory's kind of fuzzy . . ." He felt in his pocket again and produced two small squares of paper which looked like photographic prints. He leaned forward and stretched them out to me. "Always carry my camera. That's a habit of Jake's. Comes in handy. I snapped these when you and Iris were still out on the terrace."

There were two photographs, one of Sally's desk with the paper clearly visible in the typewriter, another taken down the living-room showing the slipper and the overturned vase.

"Too dark, of course," Jake was murmuring, "to have gotten a shot of Sally down in the stream bed with the balustrade over her legs. But I guess the police'd get the idea from these. Get the idea, I mean, that I was the guy telling the truth and you . . ." He pursed his lips at me. "A liar, Pete, that's what they'd find out you were."

This clinching evidence didn't affect me much. I had known from the beginning I was fighting a losing battle. I made a move to return the photographs. He waved them away.

"Keep 'em, Pete, for your memory book. I got plenty more." He turned to Martin. "There's another little matter, Marty, me boy. I kind of hate to bring up old history, but Sally mentioned something in that letter about a rather unpleasant thing you and Marietta—yes, you, beautiful—pulled a couple of years back."

He smiled at Marietta affectionately. "I have the proof of that little carryings-on. Sally gave it to me for safe-keeping. So it isn't just the murder that would break. Get it? This other little thing'd come out too. There's another murder motive right there. And even if you ducked the murder rap, you'd be up against a mighty unpleasant situation. Seems to me, under the circumstances, fifty thousand bucks wouldn't be badly missed."

Martin's face had gone very pale. He knew as well as I did when he was licked. He said, "You'll get your fifty thousand dollars as soon as I can raise it."

"Fine," Jake grinned. "That's what I like to hear. Good straight talk." He turned slyly to me. "Still feel like you're smarter than me, baby?"

I shrugged. "It's Martin's problem. Not mine. It's up to him."

"Sure. It's up to Martin. That's good straight talk too." Jake surveyed his guests' scarcely touched glasses. "Now, charming people, how's about another little snort of Scotch? After all, it's on the house. Sally's paying for it."

He crossed to the dumb-waiter and poured a strong shot of whisky. He put soda and ice in it. He carried it, smiling, to Marietta.

"Down the hatch, beautiful."

Marietta took the drink. Her fingers gripped the glass tightly. With a violent movement of her wrist, she tossed its contents straight into his face.

"Louse," she said.

Jake brushed the back of his hand across his eyes. His face was transfixed with fury, and his whole body was taut. I thought he was going to hit her. I jumped up. Then the smile came back to his mouth. He ran a hand across his cropped, wet hair.

"Well, well," he said. "Quite a shampoo Jake got." He turned his back full on Marietta and watched Martin. "Funny. That reminds me of something. Almost the most important thing, and it slipped my mind. Jake must be breaking up. Old age."

He gestured around him. "Kind of pretty suite, isn't it? But it comes awful high. And, believe it or not, I've spent all of Sally's retainer already. Me and money. It just seems to slide through my fingers. I should put myself on a budget."

He sat down again on the arm of his chair. He twirled his drink, studying it solemnly.

"I've been figuring. Until old man Johnson starts the dough rolling, we're going to have to be pretty chummy. Not that we don't trust each other, of course. But seems like we ought to stick together for a while. Now, it's nice having a plush suite like this. But we got to figure on being economical. Know what I'm going to do? I'm going to move out of here to-night and move in with Martin and Marietta."

"No." The word, coming from Marietta, was a cry. "No. You can't do that."

Jake's eyes blinked at her. He got up and went to her, bending over her, his face close to hers.

"Hey, hey, beautiful, what's eating you?"

She was shaking. Her green eyes were blind with panic. "You can't," she babbled. "You can't. Really, you can't. Martin's working. He's writing. He—he needs privacy. He needs . . . It's too small. It's too small for three. The beds —there are only two beds."

"Quiet." Jake took her trembling arms. She struggled but couldn't shake off the big hands. "Quiet, beautiful.

What you getting so hot for?" He grinned, a brash, impertinent grin. "You ain't got any objections to my sleeping with your brother, have you?"

He released her. She gave a sob. She got up and hurried to the window. She stood there with her back to us, staring out, one hand clutching the looped silver-and-green drapes.

Jake glanced after her and then shrugged. "Well, now we've got that settled, how about moving on? I'm almost packed. And since you folks don't seem to want anything else to drink . . ."

He smiled blandly at Martin. "I hope your sister's a good little cook. Jake's a fiend for an honest-to-goodness American breakfast, plenty of eggs and hot cakes."

Martin got up. His boy's face was pale and drawn. But there was still a real dignity to him. I had to hand it to Martin. He'd behaved better than I had expected him to behave. He stared at Jake, not intimidated.

He said, "I suppose, under the circumstances, I can't prevent you from moving in with us, if you want to."

"That's right, Martin," said Jake.

"But you might as well know one thing." Martin's voice was at its quietest. "If you worry Marietta, I'll kill you."

Jake grinned over his shoulder at me. "Hark at him, Peter? A rowdy family, isn't it? Always raring for a fight."

He patted Martin's silver-blond head like an affectionate uncle.

"One thing, baby. The hotel bill's waiting at the desk. While I tuck my shirt in, how's about running downstairs and taking care of it? Do that little thing, will you?"

116

CHAPTER SEVENTEEN

Jake drove off with Martin and Marietta in Martin's car. Iris and I were left standing on the curb outside the massive splendours of the Hotel Reforma. There was a mountain chilliness in the air, and the Paseo was forlorn and empty. The faint moan of accordion music drifted out from Tony's Bar, where the tourists were still beating it up. At some distance up the Paseo, red neon lights glistened out the name of Mexico's reigning movie star: "Maria Felix."

"Give you a ride back to the hotel, Iris?"

"Thank you."

We went to my parked car. As I started it, she moved away from me close to her door. There was no physical contact between us. She was wearing an unfamiliar perfume, something light and summery, that Martin probably liked. It made her seem even more alien. The street lights, passing by, brought her face and her dark hair gleaming in and out of sight. Her profile was lovely, but there was a new fragility to it, the fragility of worked ivory. She looked more mature and much more unhappy. Not like my wife. That's what a couple of months of Haven had done to her.

I said, "This isn't the sort of evening when you go home for a good night's rest. How about a drink at my place?"

"I was going to ask you," she said.

I parked in the Calle Londres, took her past the hanging bougainvillæa vine and up the iron stairs to the apartment. I let her in and turned on the light. It was the first time she had been there since the day she had left me. It was curious watching her move into the living-room and drop her fur wrap on to a chair, half a homecoming, half a visit from an inhabitant of Mars.

"Find a seat," I said. "I'll get drinks."

I went into the bedroom and found rum, Coca-Cola, and limes. I made Cuba libres. Iris liked them. I put them on a tin tray and carried them into the living-room.

Iris had sat down on the Porfirio Díaz couch.

I put the tray on a massively carved coffee table and sat down next to her. She picked up a glass.

"Cubas," she said.

"Yes." I felt suddenly embarrassed that she would think I was using the familiar drinks in a sentimental attempt to revive the past.

"Martin hates Cubas," she said. "He says the Devil is American and invented everything that ends with Cola."

"He probably did."

She turned to me quickly. "Peter, what can we do?"

"When you're playing poker, can you beat four aces with two pairs?"

She shivered. "It's bad, isn't it?"

I said, "If you're planning to make a career out of Martin, you'd better get used to things being bad."

She put her drink down and her hair tumbled forward over her cheek. I'd seen it do that a thousand times. I had always loved it. Now it gave me a pang.

She looked up at me. "You do think Sally was murdered?"

"I know Sally was murdered. I always have. So have you."

She didn't answer.

I said, "She even hired a detective to protect her. Sally was mean with money. She'd never have done that unless she was genuinely afraid. She threw a scene at my place, saying either you or Martin or Marietta was going to murder her. I laughed it off. I thought she was playing to the gallery. I guess she wasn't."

Iris sank back on the couch.

I said, "I've asked it once before, Iris. I'm going to ask it again. Did you kill her?"

She was almost calm. Her golden-brown eyes, so unlike Marietta's green ones, were steady.

"Why should I have killed her? She telephoned to tell me that she was willing to divorce Martin, that everything would be all right."

118

"She called me too," I said. "Everything would have panned out without her being murdered."

"If Sally hadn't been lying," she said bitterly. "Sally was always lying, dangling things and snatching them away. The truth wasn't in her."

I watched her over my burning cigarette. "And the truth's in you?"

"You don't believe me?"

"You haven't told me the truth yet. For example, you knew Sally was dead down in the stream bed long before Jake found her, didn't you?"

It is curious how many different silences there are. This one was dangerous, the silence before an explosion.

She said, "I've been trying to think of you as an enemy. I can't quite do it."

"Then?"

"It's all right to tell you the truth, isn't it?"

"No," I said. "I'll make you write a cheque for fifty thousand dollars."

She smiled, fleetingly. It was an unexpected time for a smile, and I realized it could only have happened because we were man and wife, because we knew each other so well and hadn't quite got used to the habit of acting in front of each other the way strangers are supposed to act.

The silence came again. It seemed even more delicately balanced.

"So?" I said. "The truth?"

"I did know she was dead. When I came in, I looked everywhere for her. I went out on to the balcony. I saw her—lying down there in the stream bed."

"I thought so."

She said passionately, "I knew she was dead, Peter. You could see by looking at her. I knew there was nothing I could do."

"I know."

"The music was coming up from the Zocalo. They were playing 'Begin the Beguine.' Somehow, that made it so awful. Music, worn-out juke-box music, the moon, the lights, the Star of Bethlehem, Taxco—and Sally lying there."

She picked up her drink, looking at her own fingers

curling around the glass. "But it wasn't the way you saw it, Peter," she whispered. "It was different."

"Different?"

"The balustrade." She looked up, her eyes shadowed with fear. "It wasn't broken."

I didn't speak.

She went on. "When I saw her, I—I put my hand on the high balustrade to steady myself. It cracked. I could tell how rotten it was. And suddenly I realized that if . . . if there'd been an accident . . . that she couldn't have fallen *over* the balustrade, not possibly." Her voice was low, pinched. "I realized that she must have been thrown over."

"So you broke the balustrade to make it look like an accident?"

"Yes, Peter."

"Why? Because you knew Martin had been there?"

"Yes."

"How?"

"The ring."

"Where was it?"

"On the balcony. Right there. I saw it gleaming. I knew he'd had it with him that morning in Acapulco. I knew he had to have been there."

"Why didn't you destroy the letter in the typewriter, see the slipper, the overturned vase?"

"I didn't notice them. I was half-sick with fear. I broke the balustrade, sent it falling down. I picked up the ring. I didn't notice anything else. I thought I was going to faint. I went to the living-room. I sat down. And then, almost at once, you were there."

"Poor kid."

"You believe me, don't you?"

"I want to believe you, so I believe you."

She got up. Her black evening gown, cut low over her breasts, rustled like a flurry of dead eucalyptus leaves in the *patio* outside.

"Martin didn't do it," she said quietly. "You can't live with a man, see him night and day, and not know a thing like that about him."

"You can't?"

She turned. Her face was obsessed. "He did go to

Sally. He told me. But he didn't drop the ring. It was a present from her to him when they were married. She asked for it back. That's why it was there."

"On the balcony floor?"

"There wasn't a scene, Peter. She was pleasant. She said she was sorry for all the fuss she caused. She said she'd give him the divorce and go back to the States."

"And when he left and you arrived, she was dead."

She flared. "Marietta was there, too."

"Earlier."

"She could have come back. Anyone could have come. The servants weren't there."

"If Marietta wanted to murder her, why didn't she murder her the first time? Why should she leave and let Martin come and return?"

"Where was she, then, all that time when Jake was waiting for her?"

"I don't know."

She tossed back her hair. "You want to believe Martin did it, don't you?"

"I do?"

We stood close together, glaring at each other, antagonistic. The white skin of her throat was working. I felt angry too. The dreadful sterility of it all swept over me. The two of us, who had loved each other so much, hating each other. Why? Because of other people, other people's lives and lusts.

Slowly the anger went out of Iris's face.

"Peter, what's the matter with us? What the hell's the matter with us? Is it Mexico?"

"The altitude?"

"I don't know. It could be."

"You don't fall in love with someone because they're eight thousand feet above sea level."

"Then—what is it?"

"Did Martin tell you about his favourite song when he was a kid?"

"No." The flicker of anxiety that always came when she felt she'd been left out of something that belonged to Martin showed in her eyes. "No, Peter."

"It's a hymn. Used to sing it myself. It goes:

"He who would valiant be
'Gainst all disaster,
Let him in constancy
Follow the Master.

"There's no discouragement
Shall make him once relent
His first avowed intent
To be a pilgrim."

She watched me curiously. "And so?"

"That's the trouble. We're all of us pilgrims, knocking each other down, stamping on each other's faces, acting like sons of bitches just so we can get to the top of our own little hills. Sally got in the way of one of us. So . . ."

"God knows what we get at the top of the hill, Peter."

"God knows."

Iris sat down on the couch again. "We certainly louse things up, don't we?"

"We louse them up."

I sat down next to her. The silence was different now, an exhausted silence, as if all the emotion in the world had been used up.

She turned to me, her lips half parted in a way that made her look curiously naïve.

"I love Martin very much, Peter. It wouldn't change the way I feel—whatever he'd done."

"I know that."

"Peter?"

"Yes."

"If Marietta had killed Sally, would you . . . ?"

"Iris, let's not talk about Marietta."

She shivered. "My love for Martin, it's—not a pretty love. It's physical, but it's never been physical. We never . . ."

"I know."

"Sometimes, when I feel shut out, when he goes off into the past, it hurts so that I almost hate him."

"Sometimes I love you, sometimes I hate you."

"Yes. I know. It's shoddy. But love's shoddy."

"Was our love shoddy?"

"I suppose so." She added suddenly, "No, it wasn't. Was it, Peter?"

I looked at her. I didn't just see the desirable mouth, the warm ivory of her skin, the curve of her bare arm, I saw all the things we'd done and said and thought and felt together.

"I didn't think so," I said.

This was another kind of silence, reminiscent, rather sad, trembling on the verge of something which neither of us quite wanted.

Iris broke it. She shrugged her smooth white shoulders bleakly. "Then there's nothing we can do—about Jake?"

"Nothing at the moment, except pay the fifty thousand dollars."

"And pay on, on, on?"

"That's for you and Martin to worry about. I'll be out of it."

She looked at me quickly. "No, you won't."

"Why not?"

"Because of Marietta. You're in love with Marietta. And she's as much in this as Martin."

I don't know why that took me off my guard, but it did. And by bringing Marietta into my mind, Iris had dispelled the intimacy. We were just two people again, two people hopelessly tied to two other people, with the shadow of murder hanging over us all.

Iris rose and reached for her wrap.

"Time I went back to that dreary hotel."

I got up too. "You don't have to leave, you know."

She turned, the coat dangling from her hand. "I don't?"

"There's no law against a wife sleeping in her husband's apartment."

Her face lightened. "I'd love to stay, Peter. At the hotel I'd feel shipwrecked. On a raft." She laughed. It was a sudden, spontaneous laugh, and I realized I hadn't heard her laugh since we were in Mexico. "But there's a practically insurmountable problem."

"Which is?"

"I haven't got a toothbrush."

"Yes you have," I said. "You left one in the bathroom. A pink one."

"Oh, that divine pink one. I bought it at Liggett's."

"Walgreen's."

"Liggett's." Iris dropped the wrap again.

I said, "About the divorce."

She swung round. "What about it?"

"Shall I still get things started to-morrow?"

She looked nonplussed, a little dazed. "I—well, maybe we should wait, just a while, wait to see what happens with Jake. You never know. It might not . . ."

"No," I said, "it might not. Then I'll hold my horses?"

"I think you'd better." She moved to me and stood close to me. "Peter, you've been so good."

"Sure."

She watched me appraisingly. "You look fine. Handsomer every day. What are you thriving on? Love?"

"Disaster," I said.

"Good night, Peter." She reached up and kissed me on the mouth, a light, cool kiss. I felt an impulse to pull her to me and make it a real kiss, but I resisted. The kiss stayed cool.

"Good night, Iris. Remember where everything is? The bathroom, et cetera?"

"Sure thing."

"When do you want to get up in the morning?"

"Oh, any time. Whenever you do."

"Good night, Iris."

"Good night." She took the bedroom. Twenty minutes later, as I lay, worn-out and half asleep, on the Porfirio Díaz couch, I thought, *Marietta slept here, right here.*

I turned over, pressing my face against the musty silk brocade.

I dreamed of Sally.

CHAPTER EIGHTEEN

Next morning I drove Iris to the Guardiola to change her clothes. After breakfast we went to Martin and Marietta's, not for any specific reason, but because we were inevitably drawn there.

Martin's apartment was somewhere behind the Bellezas Artes Palace in a district I didn't know. It was in one of those new, vaguely German, modernistic buildings which are springing up all over Mexico City. The construction could only have been a few months old, but the stucco was already peeling off the walls, and someone had broken a pane in the fancy glass and iron door.

At the apartment Marietta opened the door to us. She was wearing an apron. I had never thought of her in a domestic role. It didn't go with her. It wasn't believable.

She greeted us casually. She was in one of her abstracted moods which were so exasperating for me because they made her as inaccessible as the peak of Popocatepetl. She seemed perfectly serene, almost bored.

"Come in. Jake's in bed. Martin's out."

She led us into the little living-room. It was shoddy enough, a few wispy geraniums on the broad window sill, some cheap modern Mexican tape chairs and a red-and-white striped studio couch. The sheets, resting on it in a neatly folded pile, showed that Marietta, the inveterate couch-sleeper, had spent the night there.

A little kitchen stretched to the left. In the rear wall was a door which led presumably to the bedroom.

Marietta said, "I'd better look at the coffee," and went into the kitchen.

Jake's voice sounded boomingly from the bedroom. "Do I hear visitors? Come on in and say good morning to Jake."

The sleazy intimacy of it all was horrible, Marietta in an apron fixing coffee in the kitchen and Jake's voice drawling from the bedroom.

Iris and I went into the bedroom. There was nothing much there except a chest of drawers, a built-in closet, and the bed, large and low with a yellow tufted spread.

Jake, bare to the waist, was lounging in the bed, propped against the pillows. A breakfast tray was balanced on his lap. He was smoking a cigarette, dragging at it with his big arm crooked at the elbow. He stretched voluptuously, making the tray wobble, and grinned at us.

"Hey, Iris. Hey, Peter. This is the life. Wonderful little cook, Marietta."

We didn't say anything.

"Happen to have a morning newspaper, Pete?"

"No," I said.

"Feel like running out to the corner and getting me one?"

"No," I said.

He looked reproving. "Now, now, temper."

Iris said, "Where's Martin?"

"Martin?" The blue eyes fixed her face. "Never sleep with that guy. He hogs the sheets. I sent him out to see the lawyer. Gotta pester lawyers or they never come out from under their cobwebs."

He twisted around, humping the bedclothes with his hip and yelled, "Hey, Marietta, how's that second cup of coffee coming along?"

Marietta appeared with a cup of coffee. She took the dirty cup off the tray and put the fresh one down.

Jake clamped his brown fingers around her wrist and grinned up at her. "Hey, what about cream? You know I take cream in my coffee, beautiful."

Marietta pulled her arm away. She went out and came back with a pitcher of cream. She put it on the tray. She looked at him with a long, steady, green look.

"Cream," she said.

Jake poured the cream into the coffee, ladled in sugar, and started to drink it. He slapped his lips over it like a man in a coffee ad relishing the rich, toasted flavor to the last drop.

"Good," he said. He turned to Marietta. "Cleaners bring my suit back?"

"It's over there on the chair."

"Fine." He put the cup down and made shooing gestures at us with his big hands. "Now, skat, all of you. How's Uncle Jake going to dress with a bunch of beautiful dames kibitzing?"

Marietta picked up the tray. Iris and I went out of the room. Marietta passed us and went into the kitchen. We could hear the clatter of the dishes being washed. Even there in the living-room the atmosphere of Jake stretched out to us. His huge, sun-tanned body seemed to be everywhere, at your side, behind you, under your feet. It was only then, in that cramped little apartment, that I felt the completeness of his control. There was nothing that could be done with him. We were tied to him as tightly as two Roman gladiators tied together with knives to fight to the death.

In the bedroom he was whistling jauntily. I could imagine his hands stuffing the shirt tails into his pants, flicking the necktie over into a knot. I could feel my loathing of him in my skin. If I'd been on my own, I'd have gone into the bedroom and beaten him, really beaten him up in judo-style. My fist felt itself crushing into his teeth. My arm was choking his neck back. My foot was kicking him in the groin.

But I couldn't do anything, of course, because I wasn't on my own. I wasn't in his power. Martin was, and Iris and Marietta.

The front door opened and Martin came in. Iris jumped up. He saw her and smiled. It was the same smile, liquid as quicksilver. His fair hair seemed to have brought in the sunlight. Martin wasn't crumpling under disaster the way I had somehow expected him to. He was still the golden boy, but now he was the golden boy roused. The muscles of his compact body seemed to have tightened. There was danger in his calm. His pilgrimage was being threatened.

"Hello, Iris," he said.

"Martin." She ran to him anxiously.

"What happened, Martin?"

"I've been to see Johnson."

"I know."

Jake appeared in the bedroom door. He was in his shirt sleeves. His pants were supported by a bright pair of red-and-white embroidered braces.

"What'd he say, Martin?"

Martin ignored him and spoke as if he was talking to the air. "I told him I had outstanding debts that had to be settled. I made him see it was important. He says he might be able to get part of the money for me in a week."

Jake's lips stretched, showing the white teeth. "Attaboy."

"You're going to get your money." Martin still didn't look at him. "So you'll oblige me by clearing out of here immediately. And don't let us see your repulsive face again until it's time to pay you off."

Jake blinked. "Well, well," he said.

Martin sat down on the couch and lit a cigarette. "I'll phone you when the money's ready. If you run low before then and ask very nicely, perhaps we'll give you a peso or two for a beer. Now run along. I want to work."

Jake put his hands on his hips and watched Martin with mock gravity. "Hark at him. Kind of high and mighty, isn't he, for a guy who cleaned up two million smackers by murdering his wife?"

"I don't share your passion for being crude." Martin's voice was very quiet and English. "But you might get the drift of what I mean if I say you bore me. So put on your coat and clear out—if you own a coat."

The clash between them was moving underneath a quiet surface. There was no physical threat in the air. Jake strolled to the couch. He sat down, his big thigh crowding Martin's, intimately near.

"Hey, fellow, seems we got to get this straight. I'm not leaving. I like it here."

Martin drew his knee away.

"Yeah, Martin. I like it here fine. If I moved out, I'd maybe move to the police station. Wouldn't like to think of me doing that, would you?"

"If you go to the police," said Martin, "I'll tell them you tried to blackmail me for fifty thousand dollars."

"You would?" Jake's mouth drooped at the corners. "Then you and your sister and your girl friend would be wanted for murder and I . . . Pretty easy to explain how I strung you along with a fake blackmail threat, isn't it? What's a little blackmail in Mexico, anyway? After all, it was just a test. If you and your harem had been innocent, you wouldn't have been willing to pay me." He gestured with his hands. "You are willing to pay me. Okay, Martin." He patted the boy's stiff shoulder. "Feel like enjoying my company a little more now?"

Iris, her face white with distaste, said, "It's no good, Martin. He's got to stay if he wants to."

Martin sat leaning forward, his arms balanced on his knees, looking down at the floor. He didn't speak.

Jake patted his shoulder again and got up, grinning at Iris. "That's it, Iris. One thing about women. They got more sense than men. Martin, Marietta and me's going to get plenty fond of each other before we're through. You too and Peter."

He turned to me. He changed his attitude as if he were talking to a friend. "Peter, my boy, I'm sorry about dragging you in on this. After all, I know you're as innocent as a lamb. But then, I figured you'd rather tag along, seeing that you've got an interest in the welfare of these two lovely ladies."

"You mean I won't turn you into the police because I know it'll be Iris and Marietta who have to pay for it?" I asked.

"Something of the sort."

"Don't worry," I said. "I'll stick around—even at the expense of having to look at you."

He pouted. "Now, Peter, is that nice? Maybe it's a plain mug, but the tomatoes go for it." He winked at Iris. "Maybe it's jealousy, Peter. Shouldn't be jealous, you know. That's not manly."

He started rolling down the sleeves over his thick arms and buttoning them at the wrists. "Now we've brought up the subject of sticking together, I'm getting kind of fed-up with Mexico City."

"You are?"

"Yeah. First place, this dump's too small for the three of us. And there isn't room for you and Iris. Mexico's quite a city, too big. If we don't stick together maybe some of us'll get lost."

"Meaning that Iris and I would take a powder?"

"Oh, no, Peter. I don't think things like that about you. Deserting your friends? But . . . well, I figure we'd have a better time if we moved to a smaller place, somewhere we could all be together and be quite sure there's no double-crossing going on until that money comes through." He was looking at his square hands. The fingernails were rather dirty. "There's a carnival starting in Veracruz. Know that?"

"No," I said.

"Quite a carnival. Mexico's Mardi Gras. The biggest thing in carnivals. I think we might all move down there, join in the festivities while we're waiting for Mr. Johnson. How's about that for an idea?"

I said, "Is this a command?"

Martin, his face dark with ferocity, got up and said, "We're not going any damn place with you."

Marietta had appeared at the kitchen door. She had taken off the apron. She stood there, leaning on the lintel. Her dark hair gleamed against the white woodwork. She was watching the back of Jake's head with green, unfathomable eyes.

"Oh, yes, Martin," she said, "we are going to Veracruz for the carnival. The louse says so. We have to do what the louse says."

Jake swung round. His face was flushed. Marietta was the only one who could rile him.

She smiled at him, the sudden, Haven smile. "You don't like being called louse, louse, do you? How much are you going to charge me? Fifty thousand a time?"

She pushed past him and went to Martin. She took his hand. "Martin, darling, don't get angry. It's no good. Life's going to be hell anywhere so long as he's around. Why not let it be hell in Veracruz?" She turned and looked at Jake. "Right, louse?"

They were standing close together. Their faces were close together. Marietta's head was tilted upward. Her dark lips were half parted in a strange secret smile. It was almost as if her hatred was a kind of intimacy between them. The old discredited image came again of the two of them in Acapulco where they had never been together. I saw the two bodies on the beach. Jake flagrantly desirous, Marietta, hating, yet drawn to him like a doom. It hadn't happened, I knew. And it couldn't ever happen. Marietta couldn't . . .

Jake was looking at her in silence. Suddenly his lips moved into a smile too. It was a smile of some sort of triumph. He said softly, "I don't think it's going to be hell for you in Veracruz, beautiful. I think you're going to enjoy it."

"You do?"

"I do." He brushed past her to Martin. He said, "You can make arrangements to have the money sent to a Veracruz bank, can't you? All it needs is a letter to Johnson."

"I suppose so."

Marietta was always an enigma to me, but usually Martin was open as a book. I could tell now that what was killing him was that his independence was being impinged upon. Whether he himself had murdered Sally or not made no difference. Jake had evidence at least to put him in prison. Jake had him where he wanted him. And never before in his life, with his train of adoring women, had Martin been dominated by someone else. Jake, with his intrusive masculinity and his subtle flick of the whip was the Enemy to him, as a tiger-tamer is the Enemy to a tiger fresh out of the jungle. Even his body was rebelling against him. Neither Iris nor I nor even Marietta was as dangerous to Jake as Martin. And he knew it.

He was watching Martin calmly. He murmured, "One thing, baby, we'd better get straight, one little thing. Just in case you're getting ideas, I wouldn't kill me if I were you. Know why?"

A shiver ran through Martin. He didn't speak.

"No, baby. Don't try to kill Uncle Jake, because Uncle Jake doesn't like being killed. Know what I did last night? Wrote a full report of the discovery of Sally's body, including everything I noticed about the condition of the balcony. Not only that. A full report of Sally's hiring me, too, and an outline of why she needed protection. Needless to say, I explained my reasons for suppressing evidence. I intended to use my position as your friend to trap the murderer. Oh, yes, there was a little pen picture of you and Marietta and Iris too. I wrote all that. Sent it to a Mexican lawyer I know in Taxco with quite simple instructions. Told him that if an accident or anything happened to me, he was to deliver the whole works to the Captain of Taxco Police."

Martin just stood. I couldn't tell whether he had been listening or whether he needed all his powers to keep his passion in check.

But I had listened. And I saw then that Jake had given the final closing tug to the net. Before, there had been that one desperate solution of killing him. Even that was gone now.

Marietta was still close to Jake. She said quietly, "The evidence Sally had against Martin and me . . . in the past. Did you send that to your lawyer friend too?"

"What d'you know?" exclaimed Jake. "There I go forgetting things again. No, beautiful. I got that right with me. Meant to hand Martin a sales talk on that little item. How much d'you suppose it's worth? Ten thousand, maybe? But that's something we can discuss later in Veracruz. No point in rushing things."

"No," said Marietta. "There isn't."

There was a bowl of tropical fruit on the side table. Jake strolled over and bit into a pomegranate. The juice, red as blood, stained his mouth.

"Well, folks. Guess everything's fixed up, isn't it? How's about starting for Veracruz in an hour? That gives you plenty time to pack. And don't worry about accommodations. Trust Jake. I reserved five rooms at the Colonial last night."

I didn't exactly understand why he wanted to move us to Veracruz. There was a reason, of course. There was always a reason behind anything he did. But I did know, of course, that we would have to go.

I said, "Come on, Iris. We'd better get started."

She half turned to Martin. He didn't seem to notice her.

Jake was saying, "Hey, Marietta. What is this place? A tavern? Do you have to order your drinks around here? How's about a nice cool beer for Uncle Jake."

As we left, I thought how Sally would have enjoyed this. Martin, Marietta, and Iris were the three people she had hated most in the world. All the evil she might have wished on them couldn't have equalled this. She seemed so close that she was almost at my side. Tiny, with the heavy weight of blonde hair, the little restless hands, and the eyes sparkling with malice. I could almost hear that light, pretty voice.

Really, Peter, this is worth being dead for.

CHAPTER NINETEEN

Martin, Iris, and I were sitting in an outdoor café on the Zocalo, waiting for Marietta and Jake to come from the hotel. We had been in Veracruz five days, and the carnival was at its peak. Our table was on the edge of the seething sidewalk. Clusters of figures in tall-hooded black dominoes danced by through the blue evening light, clutching each other and shrilling in the high, batlike twitter of the carnival. There were wild papier-mâché masks—masks with red, bulbous noses, masks with drawn, tragic mouths. Peasants from the country streamed past in bright traditional costumes. A huge man, dressed as a bride, paraded back and forth with a doll baby in his arms. He was moaning that he had been abandoned at the altar. The whole town had become a huge tropical aviary, alive with bird chatter and the dazzle of flashing colours.

The cafés stretched the full length of the garishly lit Zocalo, and the square was mad with sound. On the sidewalk three feet from our table, four Veracruzans in blinding white suits, with scarlet handkerchiefs knotted at their necks and bleached straw hats, were pounding a marimba. The instrument's sad tinkle warred with the thunderous cacophony of drums from deeper inside the restaurant, where a band of half-naked boys were shaking and wriggling through a Cuban rumba. Everyone was laughing and shouting. A massive blonde, who might have been an American, was weaving through the tables, dancing with an imaginary partner and singing with tuneless shrillness. She was oblivious to everything. Her eyes were glazed in an alcoholic or morphine stupor. She had been doing it for three days. No one paid her any attention.

Streamers, yellow, red, blue, hissed through the air like

134

flying serpents. They curled into people's soup and twined around the legs of the harassed waiters running with trays of beer and shrimps. It was a real carnival, a people's carnival, not a carnival for the newsreels.

For five days this insane gaiety had been our prison. We had lived through our hair-trigger relationships to the accompaniment of inebriated trumpets, full foreign laughter, and clouds of confetti. It had affected us profoundly. Even Jake was becoming jittery. He had kept us ceaselessly under observation, and I was beginning to see that he was afraid of us. Not afraid of anything we could do, because there was nothing we could do. But afraid, almost spiritually, of the constant and implacable hatred that he had brought into being.

The rest of us were changed too. A carnival can be faintly awe-inspiring at the best of times to an onlooker. For us, who were far from participants, it was almost sinister. In Mexico City, although I had known that either Martin, Marietta, or Iris must have murdered Sally, the real enormity of the crime of murder had not registered. Here it was different. After a few days, I became obsessed with the thought, *One of them is a murderer.*

I watched them in a new way, with a kind of dread, waiting for a turn of the head, the movement of an eyelid, that might betray the guilt which had to be inside one of them.

I think Iris was feeling the same way. She was quiet, almost apathetic, hardly conscious of me. And Martin daily seemed less and less conscious of her. His almost sullen indifference was hard for her to bear, I knew. But then, Martin was changing more than any of us. He seemed to be retreating farther and farther into himself away from an existence he refused to lead. He didn't write. He hardly ever spoke. He came alive only sometimes when Jake and Marietta were with us. Then he would watch Marietta for seconds on end with a blue, challenging fixity which was ominous.

For it was Marietta, more even than Jake, who had become the focus of our complex of emotions. Of the four of us, she was the only one who had not been defeated. On the surface she was much as she had always been, hauntingly beautiful, unresponsive, apart in some private dream. Sometimes she would walk away from us to spend hours sitting alone on one of the long, grey breakwaters that fingered out crookedly into the windy Gulf. Sometimes she would bring a café to life with a bout of sudden gaiety. She ignored me almost entirely. And, although she was always aware of Martin, she hardly ever spoke to him. Her whole orbit moved around Jake. When he wasn't there, she watched for him with a green, patient gaze. When we were at a table, she always sat next to him. Her hand was always close to his on the cloth. And every now and then her eyes, intimate as lips, would linger on his brutal, handsome face.

I was sure of her loathing for him. But there was so much more that I could not be sure of. Martin felt it too. I could tell that. And Martin had reached his own decision as to what was between Marietta and Jake. That explained the blue, fixed animosity of his stare.

The marimba had hammered into "La Barca de Oro." One of the boys was singing in a deep voice, sweet with nostalgia. The jungle beat from the drums inside the café warred against him with its conflicting rhythm. But the voice soared above it, pure and sad. I didn't hear the voice. In my mind I heard only the wheeze of the Taxco pipe organ playing that same tune while I looked down through the broken balustrade at the silver rag doll that was Sally. The rowdy abandon of the carnival was suddenly touched with the chill of death. Sally seemed everywhere in the café. Sally laughing, letting the heavy hair pull her head back, Sally having her revenge.

I ordered another round of Cubas. I could feel the uneasiness in Martin and Iris, sitting silently opposite me. I was uneasy too. When we left the hotel, Marietta had still been out somewhere down on the breakwaters. Jake had been having a bath. He had said he would join us with Marietta at the café. That had been almost two hours ago. I was thinking of Jake and Marietta alone at the hotel. Martin and Iris were thinking about it too. The three of us were tied together by so many subtle threads, love, frustration, fear. In this new, artificial closeness, I could often read their thoughts as easily as my own.

The waiter brought the drinks. A little boy selling peanuts tugged gently at my sleeve and hissed to attract my attention. I had sent him away a dozen times before. I paid him no notice.

Suddenly Martin said, "A letter came from Mr. Johnson to-day."

I looked at him sharply. "What did he say?"

A woman selling a hammock spread it out in front of Iris. A man swaggered by with a peacock tucked under his arm. The *mariachi* was moaning:

"Adiós, mujer, adiós para siempre . . ."

Martin said, "He's making arrangements to send a draft to the bank. The money should be here to-morrow."

"How much?"

"Enough for Jake."

Iris's face lit up. "Then to-morrow it'll be over?"

"Theoretically."

From the café next to ours, I could hear the ponderous slop-slop of feet dancing one of the local peasant dances. It and the marimba and the rumba and the laughter and the clatter of glasses.

"It had better be over," I said.

"If it isn't?" asked Martin.

I had visions of endless weeks shackled to Jake while Sally's fortune gradually slipped through Martin's fingers into Jake's pocket, endless weeks of frustrated intimacy, with Iris loving Martin, my loving Marietta, and Marietta . . . ?

"We'll do something," I said.

"What?" Martin's eyes were bright. "Kill him? How can we kill him with that letter waiting for the police in Taxco?"

I said, without much conviction, "We'll do something."

There was a tug, like a tug of a little, weak fish mouth at my other sleeve. A tiny girl stood there, hopeful-eyed, with a box of chewing gum.

"Cheeclets," she piped. "Cheeclets."

A new rattle of drums and a twang of guitars sounded ahead of me. I looked up. Yet another band of dancers was pouring through the tables. I could see shrill magenta turbans, sparkling spangled brassières, white, gleaming teeth, and bare, honey-brown stomachs. The whole

137

café seemed to quake to this new eruption. The dancers writhed from table to table, rotating their hips, dropping into patron's laps, twining their golden arms around necks, kissing strangers, and laughing their deep, husky laughter. Behind them, keeping up the relentless rhythm, moved the instrumentalists dressed in scarlet and white. The party, roaring with sound, streamed to our table. A man in a pink, puffed-sleeved jacket of feathers was clutching a grass-skirted figure from behind with his hands tight against the bare skin of the midriff. They quivered together in a sort of tawdry ecstasy. Then the figure in the grass skirt twisted away. It moved lasciviously toward me. I saw the grotesquely full vermilion lips. I saw the copiously stuffed artificial breasts. And I realized he was a boy. All the wildly dancing girls were boys.

The first dancer slid into my lap. He kissed me on the ear. He leaned across the table, ruffling Martin's hair and laughing. A hailstorm of multicoloured streamers tangled around us. A cloud of confetti descended like rain. The boy's body was hot and sticky with sweat. It pressed down into my thigh. The little girl tugged at my sleeve again and almost whispered, "Cheeclets . . . Cheeclets."

Suddenly Martin got up. He said, "Let's get away from here."

"Where shall we go," asked Iris. "To the hotel?"

"God, no. Not to the hotel. Anywhere. Let's walk."

I had given the dancer fifty centavos. He had leaped from my knee and joined his feathered partner again. They were wriggling face to face, the "man" crouching to his knees and slowly writhing to an upright position. All the other noises of the café joined the blare of the drums in an insane bacchanal. I agreed with Martin. I'd had enough myself.

I tossed five pesos on the table for the waiter. I followed Martin and Iris out on to the sidewalk.

We had abandoned Marietta. We had tacitly admitted that she wasn't going to come to us, that she had deserted us. That in itself was a terrific change. But none of us mentioned it. And none of us had an active plan.

We drifted through the Zocalo. Gleaming paper lanterns swung from the dark oiled leaves of the tropical trees. A sudden silver waterfall of fireworks cascaded from the tower of the church. A party of black dominoed figures joined hands and danced around us, gibbering and twittering. I couldn't tell whether they were men or women. A single green balloon floated past with a forlornly dangling string. Music sounded from the Cinco de Mayo, a couple of blocks away. We moved instinctively toward it, just because music was some sort of a goal.

Away from the Zocalo, the streets dropped into darkness, quiet, primitive darkness, the darkness of ordinary everyday Veracruz. But there were strings of sparkling lights ahead on the block of the Cinco de Mayo.

We reached the street, and there the carnival was even wilder than it had been in the café. The street and the sidewalks were smothered with bright, fantastic figures. One block down, on a jutting balcony, we could see the illuminated figures of the orchestra, playing for dancing in the streets.

We pushed our way forward, three abreast, Iris between Martin and me. People weren't dancing here, just milling back and forth, shouting, embracing, arguing, munching tortillas bought out of the skillet on little charcoal stoves at the curb. We reached the fringe of the dancers. Boys dressed as girls everywhere. That seemed to be the keynote of the carnival, as if the Mexican men, always contemptuous of women, showed them once a year that they could excel them even in physical allure. Everyone was dancing with everyone, men with men, women with women, hooded, masked, costumed or in plain, everyday blue jeans. The orchestra was pounding out "Yo no soy marinero." Its jumpy, shameless rhythm caught the very spirit of the swirling, gala street.

I was a little ahead of Iris and Martin, jostled back and forth by the dancers, when I saw Marietta. The sight of her came with a sudden impact. She stood out because she was tall—taller than the tiny Mexicans, taller and far more beautiful than anyone else. She was wearing a gorgeous Tehuantepec peasant costume. It was blue and white, its flaring skirt rich with embroidery. The low neckline revealed the soft whiteness of her shoulders. The fantastic headdress of starched white lace circled her face like a frame. The effect of that fair northern figure dressed in the tropical splendour of the Isthmus and melting into the gaiety of the street scene was somehow shocking. She was dancing. A Mexican boy, dark as brown velvet, clutched her around the waist and was swaying her to and fro. His face with its gleaming smile was close to hers. She was smiling too. Her lips were half parted. Her head was tossed back, the dark hair tumbling to her shoulders. Excitement was around her like a little cloud.

I stopped. Martin and Iris came up to me. They saw her too. Another Mexican boy had pushed the first one away and was swinging her around. A third came to take his place. And a fourth. She was the centre of a ballet of bare, golden, eager arms.

Then, as I watched, a huge figure in a scarlet, hooded domino stalked through the crowd, pulled Marietta from her partner and, dragging her close to him, rotated to the throbbing music. The inquisitional hood hid his face, but it was no disguise. The heavy breadth of the shoulders, the brash, swaggering stance gave him away as Jake.

Martin's hand gripped my arm. The grip was tight as a tourniquet. I glanced at him. He was staring straight through the dancers at Marietta in her passive splendour. His eyes were blue as blue flames. For a second his fingers dug into my arm. I don't think he even knew he was touching me. Then he ran forward through the revolving bodies, ran straight to Marietta and Jake.

Iris and I went after him. Jake and Marietta saw us. They stopped dancing. They stood watching Martin and Martin watched them. Violence was in Martin like a savage dog straining at the leash.

The embroidered breast of Marietta's dress was rising and falling from the exertion of the dance. Partly from that. Partly too from the excitement that welled up, shining in her eyes.

She laughed, a queer false laugh. "Hello, Martin. Want to dance?"

He said, "Where did you get that costume, Marietta?"

"Jake bought it for me. We decided it was absurd to be at a carnival and not dress up. We thought——"

He said very quietly, "Go back to the hotel and take it off."

Marietta blinked. "Why, Martin? Don't you like it?"

"Go back and take it off."

Jake laughed. "Being British about your sister accepting presents from strange gents, Martin? Don't worry, old horse. You're paying for it."

Martin utterly ignored him. The violence was for Marietta alone. They stood, watching each other, absurdly beautiful, absurdly alike, absurdly Anglo-Saxon, lethally antagonistic. And I knew the climax of their strange, secret relationship was coming. This wasn't just a quarrel about a dress, about the good taste of being there with Jake. This was Martin and Marietta, the brother who had demanded his sister's blind worship, the sister who had worshipped blindly and had lost him to the boy at school, lost him to Sally, lost him to God knew how many people, and who now was dancing in the street with his and her own mortal enemy. This was a Haven affair. Beyond us.

Martin repeated, "Are you going to take off that damn thing he gave you?"

"I don't think so," Marietta's voice was soft too, but quite as firm. "I don't think so, Martin."

The music and the dancers pulsed around them. A red streamer swooped through the air, falling across Marietta's smooth shoulder. Some of the dancers glanced at us. Not many. This was only one of the night's thousand dreams.

With a crudity made worse by the polite formality of his tone, Martin said, "If you hadn't whored in a bar and picked him up, this would never have happened to me."

That was cruelly untrue, of course. Sally had put Jake on to us. He would have come into our lives some way or another. But what was true didn't matter at that moment. Martin had been wrenched out of his private world of memories and words and flung into life as the rest of us had to lead it. Rebellious, he was groping for a scapegoat on whom to throw the blame for his obstructed destiny.

Marietta, who had "died" in the cowslips halfway up

the hill, had always been the scapegoat. It must inevitably have come this way. My own feelings for Marietta at the moment were almost as complex as Martin's. I wanted her. I hated the memory of the Mexican arms around her. I almost hated her for not knowing I existed.

Martin wasn't looking at his sister now. He was looking up at the orchestra on the balcony, where pots of pink geraniums gleamed behind the vivid lighted musicians.

"You picked him up in a bar the way you pick up every man who bothers to proposition you. And you want him just the way you want all the rest of them. That's how far you've gone. It doesn't matter that he's a shoddy crook, draining our blood away. He's a male, a body, he lusts after you. And you want him—like a dog wants a dog."

The words were brutal as a chisel smashing into wood.

Jake took a plunging step toward Martin. I gripped him, throwing him back. The excitement around us was like tinder. One fight and the street would catch fire.

I said, "Do you want to start a riot?"

Dimly I noticed that the music had changed. The satyr pulse of "Yo no soy marinero" had gone. A melody, sweet, slow, forlorn as the floating balloon in the Zocalo had begun. It was just a tune to me until I looked at Marietta. Then, from her face, I knew. Ironically it had come again. "La Borrachita." That melancholy song which, somehow, was the theme of her bewitched relationship with her brother.

"Borrachitá, me voy par olvidarle."

All the defiance had gone out of Marietta. Her shoulders had drooped. Inside the butterfly headdress, her face was pale, lost. Her hand went out to Martin. She said in a small voice, "Martin . . ."

"Shut up," he said.

"But, Martin . . ."

He swung round ferociously. "What do you want? Do you want me to do it? Do you want me to give it to you right here?"

He raised his hand and, flashing it forward, struck her

hard on the cheek. She staggered back against Jake. Her eyes went blind. Jake pushed her aside and leaped at Martin. I sprang between them.

Martin's eyes were still fixed on Marietta. "You've ruined everything. You've fouled us all up with your lusts and your panics. You even killed Sally because you were scared she would throw you in jail for a piddling little——"

Iris ran to him. She took his arm. She looked at him beseechingly, "Martin, please. Martin, darling . . ."

He pulled himself free of her. The wheat-blond hair fell forward over his forehead. His eyes were on fire. He looked like a man hunted by all the hounds of hell.

"Get away," he said. "All of you, perverting, twisting, hindering . . . All of you, get away from me."

He turned through the dancers.

"Martin . . ." called Iris.

Marietta stood still. Her hand moved to the red spot on her cheek.

"Martin . . ." called Iris. "Martin, come back."

But there was nothing but the dancers, body against body, dusky cheek against dusky cheek, moving slowly, almost ritualistically around us.

"Borrachitá, me voy hasta la capital . . ."

CHAPTER TWENTY

Jake glared through the eyeholes of the red hood at the spot where Martin had disappeared. His arm had slid around Marietta's waist. Her eyes were still flat as green glass, and I could see the red stain on her cheek.

Jake said, "The bastard. When I get to the hotel, I'll——"

"No," said Marietta.

He pulled her around so that her face was close against the bizarre red hood.

"Don't let it get you down, beautiful."

"No. No, I won't. I——"

"There's dancing at Mocambo. Even wilder than here, they say. How's about it?"

Iris and I might have been just any two of the dancing Mexicans for all the attention they paid us. Marietta was watching Jake fixedly now as if she could see through the scarlet hood, see the mouth, near to hers, the square line of his jaw.

Jake pulled her closer. "How's about it, baby?"

Dimly I realized that for Marietta this was a moment of immense importance. There was revulsion in her eyes, but a strange fascination too. Her bondage to Martin had reached its climax. Now it was either one thing or the other, not both.

Suddenly she yielded to the pressure of Jake's arm and to the strength of will that emanated from him. She leaned against him passively.

"Yes, Jake, let's go."

"Attagirl." He laughed the laugh of a man who had always known he would get what he wanted to get. "What's a town for, I always say, if you don't paint it red?"

They turned their backs on us. Jake pushed a path for them through the dancers.

144

Iris and I were left alone. We seemed increasingly to be left alone together. The drama swept around us and we had no part in it. We had dwindled almost to spectators.

Behind us on the corner the lights of a cantina gleamed brightly. I thanked heaven that there was always a cantina.

I took Iris's arm. "Let's have a drink."

She let me guide her through the dancers and through the grimy swing doors into the bar. It was the lowest kind of dump. It was crammed to overflowing, but most of the merry-makers seemed to prefer standing. I found a small, rickety table vacant in a corner. A waiter came. I ordered Cubas. The carnival was here as much as it was on the street. Beyond us a marimba was playing. People were singing. But I hardly noticed any of it. I was saturated with carnival.

Iris lit a cigarette, stooping over the wax match. Her hair fell forward, dark against the white skin. I had expected the scene in the street to have left her an emotional wreck. But when she looked up, her face was calm. It reminded me of the sort of serenity that comes to a patient in the hospital when she has been told that there is no more to hope, that the disease is beyond cure.

She said, "He doesn't love me any more, Peter."

I didn't speak.

"He thought he needed me. He thought I could help bring back the spark after Sally. But that was before Marietta, before all this happened. Now . . ." She shrugged. "Now I'm just part of all the sordidness, part of the thing that's holding him back."

"From the top of the hill?"

"From the top of the hill." She smiled a sudden unexpected smile. "It's funny. I know everything's over. I ought to feel it everywhere, in my arms, my legs, my bones. I don't feel anything, just a—gap."

A few weeks ago I would have given my right hand to hear that. Now it had come, here in this dirty little cantina, and to me it was just words, brushing the surface of my mind while I thought of Marietta and Jake pushing away from us through the crowd, going to Mocambo to dance.

145

I said, "It'll come later—the feeling."

She shivered. "Yes."

The marimba had stopped playing. Three of the men were carrying it out of the bar. The fourth was at our table with his huge straw hat held out toward me. I tossed twenty centavos into the hat. He went away.

Iris said, "I don't think he ever loved me. There's too much Martin Haven in him for him to love anyone else."

"He writes books."

"Yes. He writes books." She laughed. "I'll go on loving him for a long time. Funny, isn't it?"

"No," I said.

"You see, this made it all show. Anything would have been more bearable for Martin than this. It's not the money. Money really isn't anything to Martin. It's Jake. Being ruled by Jake, patronized by Jake, smiled at, teased like a chipmunk, teased by a cat. It's being possessed, almost physically, by a man. That's what's killing him. And because Martin doesn't think, he only feels, I'm part of all that to him. Part of it—and I'll never be anything else. That's why he's turned against me."

"And Marietta."

"Marietta?" Her face sharpened with anger and disgust. "Why shouldn't he turn against Marietta? Why should anyone bother about her? Martin's right. She's just a——"

"Don't say it."

That strange, passionless closeness which I had felt when we were together in my apartment in Mexico City had come again. Iris and I. I wondered if very old people who had been married many years felt like this. Impersonal, but fond.

I said, "Anything's better for Martin than this?"

"Anything. Anything."

"And you don't think Martin killed Sally?"

"No, Peter."

"And you didn't kill her yourself?"

"Do I have to say that again?"

"Then why did you let this go on? Why didn't you go to the police? Martin didn't do it. You didn't do it. What did you have to lose?"

She watched me steadily. "I didn't dare."

"Because you were afraid Martin might have done it after all?"

"Because I was afraid they would think so."

"And why do you suppose Martin didn't go to the police if he's innocent and if life is so intolerable to him this way?"

A faint flush showed in her cheeks. "There is this thing he did in the past. Jake has evidence of that. Martin knew that even if he wasn't accused of the murder, they'd put him in jail." She looked at her drink. "Peter, why didn't you go? To the police? You were never involved at all. Even Jake never pretended you could have done it." She shrugged. "That's a foolish question, of course. It was for Marietta."

"And you," I said.

"Me?" There was genuine surprise in her voice, surprise and a kind of pleasure as if I had complimented her. "You mean you could still worry about me—after the way I've behaved?"

"I'm not Emily Post."

Very quietly she said, "In the street just now Martin accused Marietta of killing Sally."

"That was only talk."

"You think so?"

"Yes."

"And you, Peter? Do you think Marietta might have done it? Do you?"

Marietta was so near then that I could almost see her sitting at the table between us. And for the first time her life seemed to fall into some kind of pattern. She was still an enigma, but I saw there was a sort of key. Marietta was passive. Marietta had no will. Martin had broken her will when they were children, and from then on she was in a void, belonging to Martin, losing Martin, drifting to Jake like a will-less steel filing to a magnet, always drifting, reacting to other people's desires, having no aggression in her own. And I knew then, with a conviction almost strong enough to be true, that Marietta could not have killed Sally. She couldn't have thought of a thing and clung to it and carried it through. Marietta couldn't have gone to that house, struggled body against body with Sally, forcing her will on the other woman, pressing her back on to the rotten balustrade.

I said with a suddenness that seemed to rasp the individual silence of our table, "No, Marietta didn't kill Sally."

Iris said, "So you do think it was Martin—or me?"

"I don't know."

"Peter, you do know. There isn't anyone else."

Strange as it sounds, until then I had never faced the situation that squarely. Because I knew one of them was a murderer, I had shied away from the kind of speculation that might pin the crime on one of them in particular. Marietta? Iris? Now with this new conviction that it couldn't have been Marietta, the censor was lifted. I was released into thinking. Iris's sentence stayed in my mind like a challenge. And, as I considered it, a thought came, dazzling as the cascade of silver fire from the cathedral wall. Once it had come, it seemed unbelievable that it had not occurred to me before. Excitement flooded through me.

I said, "There is someone else."

"Not . . . ?" Iris's eyes darkened with anxiety. "Peter, you don't mean that you . . . ?"

"No. Not me."

"Then—who?"

"Jake," I said.

"Jake."

"Sally hired him. She took him into her confidence. She told him all her stupid, neurotic fears that one of you wanted to murder her. She gave him the evidence she had against Martin and Marietta. He knew about the will. He knew Martin inherited everything if she died; he knew Martin and Marietta would be saved from jail if she died; he knew you would get Martin if she died."

"So he killed her." Iris leaned across the table, groping to complete the pattern. "Because we all had such terrific motives, he knew we'd be sure it would have to be one of us. He suppressed all the evidence. Maybe he even planted it. He squared the police. And he had us in the palm of his hand. He knew we'd pay for the murder he committed. He knew we'd go on until all Sally's money . . . Peter."

"It could be."

"It is, it is."

She went on excitedly. I hardly listened, because I was feeling now and not thinking. There was the relief that neither Marietta nor Iris nor Martin need be a murderer any more. I was feeling Jake too, with his crude cleverness. There was a sort of outrageous genius in the idea of killing a woman whom a lot of people wanted to kill and then blackmailing them for his own crime. Jake was exactly the type to have the genius.

If it happened that way, there was a sort of justice, too, of Sally hiring a detective as a final, malicious twist to make us suffer, Sally being destroyed by the monster she had created.

"Everything's different now." Iris was radiant with a new optimism. "We can call his bluff. All this can be over. We can go back."

Already she was thinking futilely that Martin would love her again.

I said, "We have no proof."

"We don't need proof. He bluffed us. Why can't we bluff him?" She got up. "Come on, Peter. Let's find Martin. Quick. Let's tell him."

"No," I said.

Her face fell. "Why not?"

"Because we don't have proof. Because we've got to go slowly. Because Martin hates his guts so much, we couldn't trust him."

"Yes," she said slowly. "Yes, you're right. We shouldn't tell Martin."

"Or Marietta."

She looked at me curiously. "You mean Marietta might —be on Jake's side?"

Somewhere down at Mocambo, down near the night-pounding roar of the Gulf, Marietta was dancing with Jake, pressed close against him, his hand hot against her back, his mouth near her dark, soft mouth.

"Yes," I said. "I think Marietta might be on Jake's side."

And saying that hurt as much as if I had dug a tooth-pick under my nail.

CHAPTER TWENTY-ONE

We walked back to the hotel up the Malecón. The broad water-front avenue was strung with lights. Their little reflections glowed in the dark harbour water. But all the curio stalls were closed. Hardly a person was on the street. Everyone had been drawn to the Zocalo, the Cinco de Mayo, the nerve centre of the carnival. An Argentine freighter was in dock. Its silhouette loomed black as charcoal, illuminated only by lonely riding lights. A wind was blowing in from the north. It brought flying grains of sand from the great dunes beyond the town. It skittered the fiesta flotsam, the twisted streamers, the soiled confetti—the relics of that morning's triumphant parade of the Queen of the Carnival.

After the noise, the quietness was a balm. It seemed to smooth away my uncertainty. I was sure now that I was right about Jake. In the whole group, Sally and Jake had been the only positive characters. Martin, Marietta, even Iris, were all, in a way, destined to be victims rather than protagonists. The pattern made sense with Jake, the predatory male animal, killing Sally, the predatory female animal, and with Martin, Marietta, and Iris suffering for it.

Looking back, a fatal meeting between Sally and Jake seemed inevitable. Jake with his thick, cruel wrists and his sadistic virility. Sally, small, female, bright-eyed at the bullfight, in love with death.

They fascinate me, the bullfights . . . blood and the ballet . . . dressed up for death . . .

I could see Sally, struggling in Jake's big arms, being relentlessly carried to the balcony. Perhaps she had enjoyed it. Perhaps, without knowing it, that was what she had been waiting to find at the end of her pilgrimage, a man crude as a bull to kill her.

We reached the hotel. The light showed in the transom of Martin's room. Iris veered to the door.

"No," I said.

She looked at me pleadingly. "I only wanted to know if he's all right."

"No. Better not to-night."

She obeyed me passively. I went with her to her room. She dropped down on the edge of the bed. Beneath the dark hair, her face and the skin of her throat were white. She looked like a gardenia that had been pelted by a rainstorm—drooping.

I said, "I'll handle Jake."

She looked up. "Alone, Peter?"

"He's got nothing on me. I'm on his level. It's best that way."

"You—you think we're right?"

"I'm sure we are."

"What'll you do—say?"

"Something. I'll think of something. I'm not going to rush. Maybe later to-night—or to-morrow."

"Peter?"

"Yes."

"There's still the evidence of the thing Martin and Marietta did. If you expose Jake, Martin and Marietta will go to prison."

"We don't have to expose him. The police are satisfied. He's seen to that. We've just got to get rid of him."

She got up and came to me. She put her hands on my arms.

"Peter, I'm frightened."

"For Martin?"

"For you."

"For me?"

"Jake's dangerous. If he's really killed Sally, he's dangerous."

I grinned. "I'm no woolly lamb myself."

"Be careful, darling."

"I'll be careful." I kissed her. She clung to me, tense and dry. I said, "Don't worry. Maybe after to-night, after all this is over, Martin——"

"Don't be nice, Peter. You treat me like an idiot child."

I put my hand under her chin, tilted her face up. "Isn't that what you are, baby? An idiot child?"

She smiled then, quickly, vividly. "Yes, darling. That's what I am."

She kissed me again. Her lips were warm. "What would I do without you?"

"Stick to the script," I said.

I drew away from her, patting her arm.

"Good night, Iris."

"Good night."

I started for the door.

"Peter . . ."

"Yes."

"If anything happens to-night, tell me."

"All right."

"However late. I won't be asleep."

"Okay."

"Good night, Peter."

"Good night, Iris."

Dim light fanned in through the window of my room. The strengthening north wind rattled the shade. I could hear music from the Zocalo below. The carnival was still swirling on. I didn't bother to turn on the light. I lay down on the bed and lit a cigarette. I had a job to do.

After weeks in which I had been forced, against my will, to play the role of onlooker, it was pleasant to be released into action again. But it was a different assignment. I was morally sure now that Jake had killed Sally. But I had absolutely no proof. Jake would know I had no proof. It would be my bluff against his.

I tried to work out a plan, but my thoughts strayed. The music drifting up from the square made me brood about Marietta. She was still with Jake. I could see the great, open-walled pavilion at Mocambo on the sea. The orchestra would be playing; the dancers would be pressed even closer than in the Cinco de Mayo. I could see Marietta clinging to Jake, crushed against the scarlet domino in the rotating throng. Marietta drifting on the tide of her own strange destiny, eschewed by Martin, wanted by Jake. And wanting him?

Marietta's image haunted me. I couldn't concentrate on what had to be done. I stubbed the cigarette. Better leave it till to-morrow. It was wiser, anyway, to wait, to exploit the advantage of the morning. I had no idea of the time, but I was tired. I undressed, put on pyjamas, and lay in the bed, listening to the music against my will, trying to remember what life had been like before I met Marietta.

It was later, much later, when she came. I was still awake. The door opened and closed and I could see her, slim and straight, in the faint light from the window. I knew who it was before she reached the bed, and my heart seemed to turn over. She almost ran to me.

"Peter."

She slid on to the bed. She put her arms around me. She was cold as ice and shivering.

"Hold me, Peter. Hold me."

"Marietta."

"Hold me."

I propped myself against the pillows. I drew her close. Her whole body was racked with shakes like an ague. She was still in the Tehuantepec costume, but the head-dress was gone. I could see her hair, like a shining shadow, against the white of the pillow slip. Her lips darted meaninglessly up and down my face, kissing my cheek, my ear, my eye. She was like a child, infested with night terrors, running blindly to the first human contact.

"Hold me, Peter. Don't talk. Hold me."

I stroked her hair. I kissed her cold forehead. I rocked her back and forth as if she were, in fact, a child. Gradually I could feel some of the violence subsiding.

I said, "What is it, Marietta? Tell me."

Her teeth were chattering.

"What is it, Marietta?"

In the semi-darkness, I could only see the shape of her, the outline of her shoulder, the white curve of her cheek, and a faint gleam that was her eyes. All in black and white, like a blurred spirit photograph.

Still holding her, I reached to the bedside table, lit a cigarette, and put it between her lips.

"Here."

153

Her hand came up. It took the cigarette and brought it downward in a little arc of flame. The spasm of shaking was over, but her body was still quivering.

"Jake," she said.

"Jake?"

"I've been with Jake. In Jake's room . . . Jake."

She said the name three times as if it were some dreadful rune. She dropped down so that her head was lying in my lap. She was completely quiet. The room was so quiet that the music from the square seemed to blare like a radio turned up. I couldn't see her face, I couldn't hear her, but I knew she was crying. There was something unendurable about the passive weight of her and the knowledge of that silent, desolate weeping.

Marietta had always been impervious. Marietta had walked through disaster, serene, cryptic, never demanding. Seeing her like this was wrong as thunder in January.

I said, "Nothing matters, Marietta. Remember that. Nothing really matters in the long run."

She moved her head on my lap so that she was looking at me. The tears had made her eyes luminous. In a quick, breathless voice, she said. "I've got it. He doesn't know. After he said that, I knew they were there with him somewhere. I found them in a brief case when he was in the bathroom. I threw it into the harbour. I destroyed the ticket. He doesn't know."

I said, "Threw what in the harbour, Marietta? Destroyed what ticket?"

"The bracelet. The pawn ticket."

"I don't know what you mean."

"The things—the proof Sally had against Martin." She repeated, "I took them. He doesn't know."

I said, "I never knew about that, Marietta."

She brought the cigarette to her lips. As she drew on it, the glow illuminated her face. It looked naked, violated, like a face in Poland during the German occupation.

"Three years ago, Peter. Before Martin married Sally, we had no money left. The book wasn't finished. He had to finish the book. The woman came. She was a tourist. She was horrible, grabbing, greedy, rich. She wanted

Martin. There was the emerald bracelet. Martin stole it. They never knew. They thought it was the guide. But they didn't do anything to the guide. There wasn't any evidence."

I put my hand down. I laid it on the smooth skin of her shoulder above the deep, swooped neck of the embroidered blouse.

"Go on."

"He brought it to me. I knew he'd stolen it. He told me. We had to have money to live, to keep us from being sent to the British Embassy for deportation. He didn't know what to do with it. Martin never knows what to do. I didn't know either. But I took it to Mexico City. I found a place. I pawned it. The money was enough."

The fall and rise of her shoulder under my hand was gentler.

"Sally was suspicious. Sally was always suspicious. After the marriage, she searched around in Martin's things. She found the pawn ticket. She went to Mexico City. She redeemed the bracelet. She knew then. She kept it. Somehow she kept the ticket too, tucked away. Scheming, waiting, so she could have them as an ace against Martin if she needed them. Then, after Martin and Iris went away together, she threatened him with the bracelet. She threatened me too. She hired Jake. She gave the bracelet and ticket to Jake because she was afraid we would try to get them back. Jake had the bracelet. But now they're gone. I took them. I threw the bracelet in the harbour."

She stopped speaking, bringing the silence back. Now that the tawdry story was out at last, it seemed almost insignificant to me. The only aspects that still had life were Sally's devious planned spite—and Marietta. Marietta, who always seemed so remote from action, had been the one who had stepped in and turned the spoils of Martin's feckless theft into bread and butter. And here in Veracruz, while the rest of us had been sunk in apathy, Marietta had set herself a goal. She had determined to retrieve the evidence against Martin, to outwit Jake. She had outwitted him.

A curious elation began. I said, "So all this time you've been playing Jake's game, giving him the come-on, just for a chance to get the evidence away. Poor kid, you've put up with him, let him maul you, been through all that —just for Martin."

"No." The word was bleak as a cry in the night. "No."

She pushed herself up into a sitting position. She had moved away from me. The physical contact was gone. I said quietly, "Then you did want him. Jake."

Her voice was very soft. "From the first moment he looked at me in the bar. From the first moment his knee was against mine and his hand was moving over my shoulder, hot, feeling it through the dress. Hot."

I felt lost, defeated. I said, "And to-night?"

She was shivering again. She sat huddled on the bed with her legs tucked under her, in desolate loneliness, struggling with the horror, whatever it was, that was in her.

"It'll never be different," she said.

"Things get to be different."

"It'll never be different. I'll always be the same. In the old days, it was better, you could put the blame on something else, you could be possessed of a devil, damned." She paused. "I'm damned," she said.

"Beautiful and damned? That was the 'twenties, Marietta. You can't be beautiful and damned to-day—not with atomic bombs and Mrs. Truman."

I could feel her slipping away from me. She hardly knew I was there any more. This moment was much bigger than I. What had happened in Jake's shoddy hotel room had brought her against a wall. There was only looking back now. She wasn't talking to me, she was talking herself back. I waited for the enigma to go, almost afraid.

"It's Martin," she said. "I'm damned because of Martin."

She was looking down at some point in the darkness of the bedspread, looking fixedly, as if, somehow, the key to her life was there, embroidered on it, if only she could find it.

"Ever since I can remember, I loved Martin. It wasn't just love. When I was a little girl, Martin and living seemed the same. Martin was the sunshine, the summer, warm winter afternoons in front of the fire cooking chestnuts. Martin was me. Just being me was Martin."

She dropped back against the pillows and looked up at the shadowy white of the ceiling. Her face gleamed pale.

"It was the same when I grew up. Oh, it was more bitter then, because I knew I could never hold him. I lost him first to boys at school, then later to girls. There was always someone else he was dazzling. But then, he dazzled me too. It was the same. There were lots of boys in love with me. Nice boys, good family, boys my mother would have liked me to marry, the sort of boys who invite you to the Hunt Ball and kiss you in the conservatory. But I couldn't. I couldn't let them touch me. When they touched me, it was like a desecration—because my skin, my blood, everything, wanted Martin."

I let my hand move to her soft, cold cheek.

"It's like being a mother," she whispered. "A dreadful kind of mother, with Martin my son, wanting him, not letting him get away, and he not really wanting to get away from me."

I said, "You don't have to tell me, Marietta. I know."

"Know? How can you know?"

"I know you, don't I? I've been with you. Do you think I'm blind?"

Her hand came up to mine, gripping it. "Let me tell. I've never talked about it. Never. Let me tell you."

"Okay, Marietta."

"It was the same, later, when we moved to London, Martin and I. Worse. I grew so I was afraid of being alone in a room with a man, afraid that he might touch me and I would scream." She shivered. "I knew it was ugly then. I knew that the thing which had seemed so shining and wonderful was ugly. And I knew that Martin would never help. He needed me loving him. It was something steady, going on and on behind the glamour. Someone he didn't have to keep up a front with, be physical, be the golden lover. He didn't care that it was destroying me. Martin doesn't care."

She stopped speaking. Music still trailed up from the square. It seemed bittersweet, false.

I said, "And when did the next thing come?"

"What next thing?"

"The wrists. The wrists with the red hairs on them?"

"You *do* know!" she breathed. "Don't you?"

"Sort of."

"It was in London. I'd been to a ball with Martin. He'd left me, gone off with some woman. A man wanted to take me home, but I slipped away. I was going home alone. It was very late. There was an all-night coffee stand. I stopped for some coffee. A man was having coffee too, just one man. He was a lorry-driver. His lorry was parked by the curb. I saw his hands first, curved around the cheap white china cup, big hands, coarse, square, oil stained, with broken fingernails. His shirt sleeves were rolled up. His arms were thick and hard like tree roots. His shirt was dirty around the neck. I could see the band of dirt. The shirt was open. I could see the bare skin, little golden hairs. And suddenly something happened to me. He looked at me and he knew. Right away, although I was in an evening dress and a wrap, he knew. He paid for his coffee. He didn't say anything to me. He went to his lorry and he waited for me to follow him. I followed him. I climbed up on to the seat next to him."

The grave English voice moved quietly on.

"He drove out of London into the country. He never spoke. He never looked at me. He kept his eyes all the time on the road. The seat was narrow. His thigh was pressed against mine. His arm was against mine. His skin through the shirt seemed warmer than any skin I had ever felt. I could smell sweat."

She waited.

"It was a desecration, of course, but it was somehow a release too. Because there was nothing of Martin here. This wasn't Martin any more than an animal was Martin. He stopped the lorry. There was darkness everywhere, no lights. He didn't make love to me, no pretence, no romance. He twisted around, he grabbed me toward him. His arms were like steel, like some impersonal power. The hotness of him seemed almost to burn me. I felt a kind of wild excitement as if a spell was breaking. And then——" Her voice shrivelled. "I couldn't, Peter. I wanted to. It seemed as if it would be salvation. But I couldn't. I started to shiver. I was in his arms, shaking, out of control. The thing for Martin was still there, you see, deep, deep inside, rebelling. There wasn't any more. He must have hated me, despised me. But he didn't say anything. He drove me back to the coffee stand. He left me. That was all."

Her hand reached through the darkness and took mine. It seemed fragile as a bird. I didn't say anything. It was better to let her go on.

"I remembered him. That night was never out of my mind. But I remembered half-fascinated, half-terrified, the way you remember ether after an operation. There'd be other men I'd see, dock hands down on the docks, labourers out in Hertfordshire, stripped to the waist, bringing in the harvest. But after that time I didn't try any more, try to break away. Things were going bad for Martin, anyway. And when things were going bad he always needed me. He'd even be nice, going away with me alone for the week-ends. Letting the telephone ring. It was nineteen thirty-nine. Everyone knew the war was coming. Dread of it hung over everything. And Martin had spent all his allowance and mine. I never knew how he spent it. Money always went, and there seemed nothing to show for it. That's when the trouble was bad. Martin did something, tampered with a birthday cheque from an uncle, tried to make it larger. It was stupid. Everyone saw through it at once. They hushed it up, of course, but the family was through with him then. Father's awfully rigorous, moustaches, honesty, Charter-house. They disinherited him. They said they would pay his debts and give him passage money if he'd leave the country. Of course, that was my chance. I could have let Martin go, sided with the family. But I didn't. When I told Father I was going with Martin, he had no use for me, either. So we came to Mexico, Martin and I. Martin was frightened. Life had caught up with him for the first time. And, because he was frightened, he clung to me. The first years here, before Sally, there wasn't anyone else. Just Martin and me. He started the book. We'd never dreamed, either of us, that he could write. But he started it, and with the book it was almost the way between us that it had been when we were children. Almost."

My heart was bleeding for her. I understood so much now, the lost green eyes, the radiance when Martin was nice to her, the terrific wound of his contempt, her pitiful searchings through me, Jake, to find some way out of the trap.

I said, "And then Sally came."

"Sally knew. She always knew things like that. She wanted Martin all for herself, and she knew I was the only danger. Martin wanted me to live with them after the marriage. Sally wouldn't let me. There were terrible scenes. I went off to Mexico City. Once I'd left Martin, father started sending me money, through the Embassy. Not much. Enough to live on. It was terrible, after Taxco, to be without Martin again. You see, in Taxco I'd let myself slide, pretended it was beautiful between Martin and me. But when I was alone again, I knew it wasn't and I tried to break it. I lived in bars. Every night there was someone, Mexicans, tourists, anyone, but it never changed. Then, that night at the Cucaracha, I met you. I ... oh, what's the use?"

I moved nearer. I put my arm around her. Her elusive perfume drifted to me through the darkness. Her body was quiet and heavy with weariness.

"Tell me, Marietta."

"I met you," she whispered, "and you weren't Martin. I talked to you and I wasn't talking to Martin. I looked at you and I wasn't looking at Martin. When you touched me, there wasn't the recoil or the other thing—the lorry-driver thing. It was right. I thought it had happened at last. But it hadn't."

"It hadn't?"

"You were in love with Iris. Iris of all people." She laughed. "Martin had double-crossed me again."

She lay quiet in my arms. Those few minutes of self-revelation had brought her as near as if I had known her all my life. The barrier she had put up wasn't there any more. I could feel her despair almost like my own.

She said in a chilled voice, "Then Jake."

"The lorry-driver," I said.

"The worse he was, the stronger it came. Seeing him get Martin into his grip, seeing him bully Martin, having him bully me, treat me like dirt, outwit us all. I hate him

and yet I want to feel the beastliness of his hands on me."
She shivered. "There's two horrors now. The horror of
Martin. The horror of this other thing. Scylla. Charybdis.
They'll always be there. I'll always be between them,
drifting to this one, drifting to that one." Her voice choked
into a sob. She twisted around burying her face against
my shoulder. "If you only loved me. If only you could put
up with me. But who could? Who could?"

She was crying, not hysterically now, but with the
hopeless steadiness of exhaustion. It was strange how vividly, in spite of the darkness, I was conscious of her
beauty. I held her closer. Her soft hair brushed my forehead. Her lips, wet with tears, found my cheek. I felt oddly
triumphant, as if this moment had been inevitable. The
end of Marietta's dark, dreadful pilgrimage?

I said, "But I do love you, Marietta."

"Peter."

"I love you."

"Then marry me. When this is all over, marry me. I'll
be all right. With you I swear I'll be all right. Marry me."

CHAPTER TWENTY-TWO

Someone knocked on the door. Marietta stirrred in my arms. I called, "Who is it?"

"Iris."

"Okay. Just a minute."

I whispered. "Stay here, Marietta." I slid off the bed. I grabbed a robe and found my slippers. I went out into the corridor, closing the door behind me.

Iris was in a white wrap with her hair loose around her shoulders. She looked at me anxiously.

"You didn't talk to him yet, did you?"

I couldn't switch that quickly from Marietta. "Talk to whom?"

"Jake."

"No, not yet."

"He's in Martin's room. Their voices through the wall woke me. Jake's mad about something. Martin's mad too. I'm afraid of them together. Martin hates him so much. He might——"

"I'll break it up."

She smiled her relief. "Don't let Martin——"

"Don't worry."

I left her and went down the dim hotel corridor toward Martin's room. I felt a reckless excitement. Marietta had asked me to marry her. I was the one she had sought out in the extremity of her unhappiness. If only Jake had killed Sally and I could scare him out of our lives, there might still be some sort of story-book happy ending for all of us. Marietta had retrieved the bracelet too, thrown it in the harbour. The little Taxco episode was over, dead. Even Jake couldn't resurrect it any more. There was the truth about Sally's murder. Nothing else.

Light fanned down from Martin's transom. I could hear

voices indistinctly from inside the room. I tried the door. It was open. I walked in without knocking.

Martin, in white cotton pyjamas, was sitting on the edge of the bed. Jake stood over him, his arms crossed, his big back to me. He was still fully dressed, but his gaberdine suit was mussed. There was something ominous about his stance, and, when he glanced over his shoulder at me, I saw that he was drunk. Not just full of liquor, but drunk. In spite of his steady intake of rye, I had never seen him drunk before. It coarsened his face, made his eyelids droop heavily over the blue eyes. He was furiously angry too.

Martin was just as angry. But anger was different in him, cold, restrained behind a grave surface composure, but equally dangerous. He had hated Jake before this evening's street clash with Marietta. Now I knew his hatred must be lethal.

As I entered, he was saying, "I've told you once. The money comes to-morrow. You can have it to-morrow. There isn't anything else to discuss."

"There isn't, eh?" Jake laughed. "When I'm out, you sneak into my room and snitch that bracelet, and you say there's nothing else to discuss." He swung to me. "Know what this bastard did? Stole something out of my room!"

"What do I do?" I said. "Cry?"

Martin's blue boy's eyes, so accustomed to find allies everywhere, met mine. "The thing I'm supposed to have stolen is the evidence Sally had about the stupid thing Marietta and I did in the past. I'm delighted it's disappeared, of course, and I'd have taken it gladly if I'd had half a chance. But, as it happens, I don't know anything about it."

Jake leaned clumsily over him. The red tie was askew. There was a sordid, end-of-a-debauch look to him, the brutality of a drunk coming home to beat his wife. His words spilled clumsily too. "That bracelet's going to cost you good money. You stole it from the dame it belonged to, and you're paying me for it—cold cash. Don't think you can act smart with Jake, baby. Get that into your pretty little head. I'm going to search this room and I'm going to find that bracelet if I have to strip those pyjamas off of your hide and——"

163

I said, "I wouldn't bother about Martin's pyjamas. He didn't take the bracelet. Marietta did."

Jake lumbered around to stare at me. Martin's body tensed with interest.

"Marietta?"

"Yes, Marietta." I enjoyed being able to put it that way in front of both of them. They both thought Marietta belonged to them. I was her spokesman now. "You overestimated your sex appeal, Jake. She was just stringing you along for a chance to get at that bracelet. She's got it and there's no use wasting time searching for it. She threw it in the harbour."

Jake's jaw sagged. The information had really hit him, not just because the bracelet was irretrievably gone, but because he had been so sure of Marietta. The man in me enjoyed seeing his sexual vanity crumble, even though what I had told him was only part of the truth.

"In the harbour?"

"In the harbour," I said.

"The bitch. The little conniving bitch."

Martin laughed suddenly. It was a deep laugh full of private amusement. He tossed back the wheat-yellow hair and sat there on the edge of the bed laughing.

"Marietta. Wonderful, wonderful Marietta." The laughter was still in his eyes but it was mingled more with extreme contempt. "How much did you hope to squeeze out of me for that bracelet, Jake? Another ten thousand dollars, wasn't it?"

I was surprised that Jake could be thrown so easily. For the first time since he'd come into our life, he was rattled. Perhaps the liquor in him had something to do with it, but I think it was mostly the anger. He was one of those people who, when they lose their tempers, lose their heads. I decided to snatch the advantage and put him through his paces as soon as I could get him out of Martin's room.

He leaned over Martin and gripped his shoulders with thick, blunt fingers. Martin's face paled in disgust. With a violent jerk, he freed himself.

"Keep your filthy hands off me."

Jake said, "Don't worry, baby. You and your sister, all of you's going to have my filthy hands around a long time yet. You're going to pay for this."

"Pay!" echoed Martin. He laughed. "The man doesn't exist, Peter. I'm sure he doesn't exist. He's something metamorphosed out of a penny dreadful. What was your mother, Jake? A bottle of ink? And your father? A grey little hack scribbling in a garret at a penny a line? Don't worry. You're going to be paid. To-morrow. Fifty thousand dollars. Remember?"

"More," said Jake.

Martin stiffened. "More?"

"Fifty thousand for murdering Sally. Ten thousand for the bracelet. And another ten thousand for making me mad." A travesty of the bland grin twisted Jake's lips. He held up a hand and started counting off fingers with the other. "Get it? Fifty. Ten. Ten. Seventy thousand bucks, or I report into the Taxco police to-morrow."

The change in Martin's expression was poignant. I could see his mind working. His triumph had been so short-lived. Of course, from his point of view, this was the end. The original fifty thousand had been an arbitrary sum. Jake had him completely in his power. He could raise the ante indefinitely, and go on raising it. I knew he might be able to start a successful counter-attack against Jake. But Martin didn't, Martin, lying there on the bed, hating Jake physically, like a wife hating a monstrous husband, hating him the more because for a few moments he had felt free of him.

In a thin, colourless voice he said, "All right. Let's forget it to-night. Let's talk about it to-morrow."

Jake loomed closer over him. "What's wrong with now?"

Martin shrugged. "Everything. You woke me up. It's late. We're probably keeping half the hotel up, and I'll probably never get to sleep again as it is."

His bottle of sleeping capsules stood on the table beside him. He picked it up, spilled two capsules into his hand and swallowed them with water from a tumbler.

Jake's hand shot out greedily. "Gimme one of them."

Martin blinked. "You?"

"I ran out." He laughed harshly. "What d'you think? Think only Havens take sleeping tablets, sensitive, thoroughbred Havens? Think you're the only ones that sleep bad? Gimme one."

Martin was watching him, a strange disturbance in his

eyes. "All right." He picked up the bottle, rolled a tablet into his bronzed palm and held it out. "Take it. It will cost you a peso. Exactly one peso."

Jake grabbed the capsule, fumbled in his pocket, and tossed a peso bill down on the bed.

Martin turned to me then. His eyes were brimming with affectionate, almost cozening amusement, like an English schoolboy who'd got away with putting a thumbtack on his form-master's chair.

"I made him pay, Peter. Let the news go ringing down the centuries. I made Jake pay."

Jake swallowed the capsule with the rest of the water in the tumbler. Martin, still smiling, rolled back into bed. This was far better than I had ever dreamed it could be. Now that the time to match Jake's bluff had come, Jake was not only drunk, he would be dopey from the sleeping pill.

I said, "Come on, Jake. Let's get out of here."

"Yeah." Still flushed with anger, he was glaring down at Martin. "Don't he look cute in bed, though. Think we should kiss him good night?"

Martin grinned. "Pleasant dreams, Jake. After all, you've deserved it. Something attempted, something done, you've earned a night's repose."

I took Jake's arm. He moved willingly with me to the door. In the corridor, I said, "How about giving me a nightcap? I'm out of liquor."

"Sure, sure, Peter." He'd never classed me as an enemy along with the rest of them. Basically, he was pretty stupid. He had nothing against me. He didn't wish me any ill will, therefore he blandly assumed that I wished him none.

We went to his room. The bed was rumpled, but the sheets hadn't been turned back. There was the sort of squalor that comes with a sloppy man—a pair of socks on the floor, a necktie looped over the bedrail. A dirty ash tray, spilling its contents on to a chair bottom. Some of the cigarette butts had red lipstick stains.

I thought suddenly, *Marietta was in here with him.* I tried to force the thought back.

Jake peeled off his jacket and tossed it on to a chair. He splashed rye from a half-empty bottle into a dirty glass and handed it to me. He didn't mix himself a drink. He sat down on the bed, his hips bulging it down, and started to take off his shoes.

"That Martin," he said. "Thinking he can get fresh with me."

"Silly," I said, swirling the drink in the glass.

"And Marietta." He looked up, kicking his second shoe off, and pulled clumsily at his socks. "Thought she was smart too, didn't she?"

Looking down into the raised face with its cropped red hair, its blunt, male features, its eyes smug with the assurance of virility, I realized I hated it more than any face I had ever known. He was grinning now, his sly, mentogether grin.

He said, "Don't worry, though, Peter, my pal. She got hers. She paid for every emerald of that bracelet. She won't forget Jake in a while."

I knew then what it felt like to want to kill someone. There was only one thing that kept me in control. The rooster strut was just false, the swagger overdone. I'd seen that swagger so often before in the war, boys coming back to the ship, bragging of a hot night which had, in fact, been spent alone at a movie. With a terrific sense of relief, I knew that I didn't believe him.

I said, "Maybe she'll forget you sooner than you think, Jake."

"Yeah?" The socks were off now. He was unbuttoning the shirt from his broad, sun-brown torso. It seemed to me that I had always known him like this, in an enforced physical intimacy, always on a bed, kicking off socks, stripping off shirts.

"Yes," I said. "I think it's just possible she may have forgotten you. By to-morrow, for example."

He threw the shirt back over his shoulders, tugged at it, and found he hadn't unbuttoned the sleeves. He worked on the sleeves.

"To-morrow, Peter? You dreamin' or something?"

"I'm not dreaming," I said. "You see, you're leaving to-morrow."

He wriggled out of the shirt. He looked up. His blue eyes watched me, unblinking. Then he grinned.

"You think I'm leaving you to-morrow, Pete? When

you and me's just starting to be pals? Sure, I get the fifty thousand to-morrow. But that's just the start. What's the matter with you? What you think I am?"

I said, "You're leaving to-morrow, Jake. And you're leaving without the fifty thousand dollars. You're leaving with nothing."

He just stared.

"Know why?" I said.

His eyes were glazed with liquor. There was something else too. A sort of overlay of stupidity. I supposed it was the sleeping pill beginning to work.

"No," he muttered vaguely, as if he was losing the track of the conversation. "No, Pete, old horse. Why?"

"Because the hoax is over," I said. "You can't nurse it along any more. You see, we know you murdered Sally."

"Me?" he said very slowly. "Me—murdered—Sally?" He stared down at the buckle of his belt. His fingers began to fumble with it as if he thought the belt buckle and not I was the problem. I was worried. I hadn't realized he was this stupefied. Maybe I was hopelessly ill-timed. Maybe I'd have shot my bolt and, by to-morrow, he would have forgotten the whole thing.

I said, "You killed Sally. You saw what an ideal set-up for blackmail it would give you. You slipped up to the Casa Haven after Martin had left, before Iris came—and threw her off the balcony."

"Balcony," said Jake. Unsteadily, he got to his feet. He had undone the belt button. His pants dropped in a sagging heap to the floor. He stood in front of me, naked except for the white athletic shorts, weaving slightly, like a punch-drunk boxer a couple of minutes before the knockout. "Balcony," he said.

I was really anxious now. I said, "Jake! what's the matter?"

"Balcony," he said.

He was only a foot away from me. Suddenly he lurched forward. His heavy arms flopped around my neck. His cheek jarred against mine. The whole weight of his torso fell on me. The bare skin of his body was cold, clammy. The complete unexpectedness of it caught me off balance. We swayed together. Then I fell backward.

He fell full on top of me. His arms were underneath

me. Suddenly they clutched into my back. Breath hissed from between his clenched teeth close to my neck. His whole body arched like a spring and then shut down on me in a convulsive spasm.

For one moment I was smothered under the vast, stiff weight of him. Slowly the extreme pressure relaxed. His body started to roll crazily to and fro over me, his big legs flailing back and forth. Then he was suddenly still, inert, clammy, stretched spread-eagled on top of me.

Using all my strength, I pushed and twisted and managed to release myself. I got up. I was shivering. I looked down at him. He lay quite still, on his stomach, in front of me—perfectly still, a great hunk of motionless male flesh.

I dropped to my knees. I took his shoulders. I yanked him over on to his back. His mouth hung open. The lower lip was bleeding where his teeth had cut through it. His eyes were filmed like dirty window-panes.

I took his wrist. My fingers were shaking. There was no pulse.

Music drifted faintly up from the Zocalo.

I knelt there, staring. I thought, *It's "Yo no soy marinero." That's the name of the tune they're playing.*

I thought that because I couldn't bring myself to think the other thing I had to think: *Jake is dead.*

CHAPTER TWENTY-THREE

I got up. I was quite calm now. It is easy enough to be calm once you're realized that a situation is beyond remedy. What had happened seemed as obvious as the body sprawled at my feet. Jake had been drunk, but perfectly normal. Martin had given him a sleeping capsule. A few minutes later, Jake had died in a convulsion.

The pattern was ironically the same as the pattern surrounding Sally's death. Sally had had a change of heart. She had summoned Iris and and me to let us know definitely that she was going to give the divorce and bring no police charges. Just when the situation was on the verge of straightening itself out, she had been killed.

And now Marietta had retrieved the bracelet from Jake. That episode had been closed. The money was to have come to-morrow. Even if I hadn't been able to scare Jake away without the money, I could almost certainly have persuaded him that the position was sufficiently precarious for him to take the fifty thousand and run. To-morrow might have been the end.

Now Jake was dead. The police would come. They would find one murder. Word of Jake's death would reach Taxco. His Mexican lawyer would hand over the damning report to the police there. Sally's death would be reopened.

After all the heartache and struggle, we would be plunged into a double murder charge.

I still felt sure that Jake had killed Sally. That was what made the situation so bitter. Martin had killed Jake, of course. I had seen him do it. And the futility of the act was so typical of him. Martin, who didn't think, who only felt, had endured his hatred for Jake until the disease of it had festered through to the bone. Then, blindly, mindlessly, he had turned on the Enemy. He had killed Jake with no thought of profit, of solving anything. He had killed him because he could no longer breathe, exist, write, while Jake was still alive. He hadn't stopped to consider the havoc he would cause for the rest of us. Martin, with the hawthorn staff, the nightgown, and the cheeks puffed with exertion, had never thought of anything except the end of his own ruthless pilgrimage. In the past there had always been for Martin someone else to take the responsibility. Probably, at the moment, he was blandly assured that I, Marietta, Iris, one of his bewitched worshippers, would step in and make everything all right for him.

A fleeting memory came of Marietta in my arms, pouring out for the first time the sterile horror of her life, clinging to me as her one chance of redemption. The beauty, the promise of those moments, which had been less than half an hour ago, seemed infinitely remote now.

I saw then that Martin was more destructive a force than Sally or even Jake had been. It was Martin who had finally defeated us, Martin with his golden smile and his retinue of lost ladies, Martin who brooked "no discouragement."

And Martin, at this moment, was more dangerous than the body stretched across the drab hotel carpet. Our chances for coming through this new ordeal were minuscule, but they would be non-existent so long as Martin was left to face the world unprimed.

I glanced down at Jake. I felt no more for him than I would have felt for a brief carcass in a butcher's shop. I thought of Sally's little broken body flung down in the stream bed.

Somehow, big people look much deader than small people, when they're dead.

The room key was lying on a table by the bed. I took it. I skirted Jake's body and left the room, locking the door behind me. Martin's room was two doors down the empty corridor, past Iris's room. I went to it. I knocked on the door. There was no answer. I knocked again. Martin gave me a muffled grunt of satisfaction.

I said, "Let me in, Martin. Peter."

Soon the door opened. The room was in darkness except for the faint street light seeping in through the window. Martin stood on the threshold, rubbing hs eyes and yawning like a little boy unseasonably awakened to amuse his mother's party guests.

"Hello, Peter."

I pushed past him. I turned on a light. The bottle of sleeping capsules still stood on the table by the bed. I went to the table and put the bottle in my pocket. Martin moved after me. He dropped down on the bed, yawning again, cupping his hands behind his head and smiling up at me his quick, blue smile.

"What's the matter, Peter? Need something to help you sleep too?"

The smile was ingenuous and perfectly friendly. He wasn't reproving me for having waked him up for the second time when he had notorious trouble in sleeping. There was no suggestion of resentment. I was his friend. I must have a good reason for waking him up. He was my friend. He'd do everything he could to help.

Under the circumstances, that sunlit charm was almost monstrous.

I said, "Why did you do it, Martin?"

He humped his knees up and pushed the yellow hair back from his forehead, still watching me trustingly. "Do what, Peter?"

"Jake killed Sally. I could have pinned it on him. I could have got rid of him. You wouldn't have had to pay a cent. Why, in God's name, did you kill him?"

Martin sat up. He was squatting on the bed. He nursed his knees with his hands. He watched me, his blue eyes flat, making a sudden curtain between me and what was in his mind.

"Kill him?"

"I saw you give him the capsule. I don't know where you got the poison or what the poison was. The doctors will."

He said, "You mean Jake's dead?" He paused. "Dead?"

"Very dead."

I could see the skin of his face whiten under the honey surface of sun tan. It seemed to dry and sag. His shoulders stooped. He drooped his head and stared down at the floor.

He said, "What are we going to do?"

"I don't know."

He had ignored my direct accusation, let it pass over him. Already it was what are *we* going to do? To have pressed him more would only have been to make myself sound hysterical. The potency of Martin's personality was remarkable. Things always ended like this—being played his way.

I said, "Get your clothes on. Don't let anyone in. Don't talk to anyone. Wait till I come for you."

"Where are you going, Peter?"

"To get the others."

"Marietta?" The word came sharply.

"Marietta and Iris."

He looked up. His face was gaunt, stripped to an elemental dread. "Peter . . . ?"

"What?"

His shoulders crumbled again. "Nothing. I'll get dressed."

He moved off the bed. He wandered around it in a daze, picking up articles of clothing at random and dropping them. He was like a man with amnesia who remembers dimly that you have to dress yourself but has forgotten how.

I left him, closing the door. I had no ultimate plan, but I knew that I would have to break the news to Iris and Marietta before we did anything. In this extremity, we all had to know everything, to decide upon a united front.

Because I shied from it so much, I went to Marietta first.

She was still in my room, lying on the bed. She had turned on the small bedside lamp and was propped against the pillows, smoking. She seemed to me more beautiful than I had ever seen her. Her face was quiet and serene. It was not the old impervious tranquillity that had made her masked as a Mexican idol. It was translucent, bright, as if she had been through the refiner's fire. She smiled at me.

"You might at least have a drink in your room for a lady."

I crossed to the bed and sat down next to her. She leaped toward me, putting her arms around my neck.

She said, "I'm happy, Peter."

"No," I said.

Her eyes, dark green as the ocean, deep below the sunlight, met mine baffled. It was senseless to ease the shock, just as senseless as to bowdlerize the brutality from a Scottish ballad.

I said, "Martin's killed Jake."

Her arms around my neck stiffened. Her lips half parted.

I said it again, "Martin's killed Jake."

"No," she whispered. "No, Peter, no."

She was there on the bed, but I could feel her gone from me as if the Atlantic separated us.

I didn't say anything to try and bring her back. I knew it was useless.

She got up.

I said, "Don't go to Martin. Not yet."

"I must. I——"

I took her arms. "No, Marietta. Promise me. Go to Iris. Tell her what's happened. Wait for me with Iris. I'm going to dress. Then we'll all go to Martin."

I made her look at me. Her eyes were impersonal, not seeing me.

"All right."

She left the room. She hadn't tried to deny Martin's guilt. She hadn't even questioned those few words which had shattered her future. She had accepted them like the inevitable fulfilment of a curse.

I dressed. I don't know why I was so meticulous about it, choosing the right tie, selecting shined shoes. I suppose in extremity you need all your armour, and there is a certain security about being well dressed. I went to Iris's room. Iris and Marietta were standing together by the bed, Marietta in her flamboyant Tehuantepec costume, Iris neat, almost severe, in a black suit. I knew at once that Iris had been told the news and it had almost crushed her. Danger to Martin had brought out a curious physical kinship between the two girls. Their dark eyes, the attitude of their bodies, showed the same sort of suffering. They might have been sisters.

But there was a difference. Marietta had accepted the inevitable. But there was still fight in Iris.

She came to me, "Peter, it's true?"

"It's true."

"But how? I don't believe it."

"A sleeping pill. Somehow he got poison. I saw him give it to Jake. There's no doubt," I said. "We'd better get him now."

"And . . . ?"

"I don't know. We'll have to think. I want you all to see him—Jake. I can't do this alone now. We've all got to face it and decide."

I took them down the corridor. The night was trailing off into morning and yet the hotel still seemed empty. There was no feeling of people asleep behind the closed doors. They were all out in the streets still, dancing through the soiled streamers, sneaking that last tequila, kidding themselves they were still young and beautiful.

Martin was waiting for us—fully dressed, very quiet. He seemed completely unaware of Iris and Marietta. He had eyes only for me. I said they were to come with me to Jake's room. He said nothing. They just trooped after me. I unlocked the door. They followed me in. I shut the door and put up the chain.

Jake was sprawled on the carpet. With Marietta and Iris in the room, the nakedness of the body, in its brief jockey shorts, was flagrantly noticeable. It made him human again, not just a carcass—human and dead.

Marietta's eyes moved past the bed to the ash tray and the scarlet-stained butts. She was remembering what had happened there . . . so short a time ago . . . between Jake and her. I wondered what horrors were in her mind. Iris had taken Martin's hand. He didn't draw it away, but he didn't react to her either. Marietta sat down on the bed, her back turned toward Jake. She lit a cigarette with a sharp spurt from the match. None of them said anything. The atmosphere of the room was heavy and clotted as buttermilk. They were leaving it all to me again.

I said to Martin, "I don't know when you got the poison. But I saw you give him the pill. It's no use pretending. It's no use bawling you out either. It's done. I said it needn't have happened, however you felt about him. And I say it again. I could have coped with Jake. He could have been frightened away."

Iris said, "If only we'd told you, Martin. Peter and I realized it to-night. Jake killed Sally. He killed her so he could exploit us. He . . ."

Martin didn't say anything. He didn't even seem to be listening. He was looking at Jake, looking down with his blue, childlike gaze, studying him as if a corpse was something new and strange, something to be observed.

It was Marietta who broke the silence. She didn't turn to us. But her back had dropped and her voice was somehow appalling.

She said, "That isn't true."

Iris and I turned.

I said, "What isn't true, Marietta?"

"Jake didn't kill Sally."

I felt a tingle in my skin. I saw the whole pattern beginning to change shape and I could hardly face having to listen to what she was going to say. I had made myself believe that the first murder had been something beyond our responsibility, something brutal that had come from Jake. It had been easier to accept, with Jake as a murderer who had finally been killed by Martin. That way the whole saga was at its least ugly.

I said, "Then who killed Sally, Marietta?"

For a moment, she didn't speak. The dark hair that hid her face from me was lustreless, dead hair.

She said, "Iris, when you arrived at Sally's, she was dead, wasn't she?"

Iris nodded, pale, not speaking.

Marietta went on, "She was alive when I left her. There's only that once entrance. You can't get in any other way. When I left Sally, she told me Martin was coming. I was worried for Martin. You wondered where I was all the time after I left her, before you found me in Paco's. I was waiting down the little dark alley by the church, waiting where I could see the door to Sally's house."

She paused.

"I saw Martin come. I saw Martin go. If Jake had come after, I would have seen him. He didn't. No one came before Iris, and when Iris arrived Sally was dead. So you see . . ."

"No." Iris took a step toward her. "Marietta, no."

"Yes." Weariness was like a yoke on Marietta's shoulders, pressing them down. "Martin killed Sally. I've always known it. From the beginning I've known it."

She got up then. Slowly she moved to her brother. He stood watching her.

"They've got to know, Martin," she said. "It's gone too far. They've got to know now."

Martin with his golden hair, his destructive boy's simplicity, Marietta, dark, doomed like Alcestis through the thing she loved.

She put her hand on her brother's arm. "To-night you accused me of killing Sally. You did that—when you knew it was you. But don't worry. I don't mind, Martin. You can't ever do anything to me that I would mind."

She paused. "And there's nothing to be afraid of, because it'll be all right for you. I'll take the blame. That way's better for me, anyhow."

"No, Marietta," I said.

She was still looking at Martin. "That way's better for me. It's the way I want it to be."

The words were bleak, final.

I had a vision of a dark little girl throwing herself down to "die" in the cowslips while a golden little boy ploughed upward with his hawthorn staff, singing . . .

CHAPTER TWENTY-FOUR

I couldn't let it happen that way. I knew it was useless to argue with Marietta. She was set on her path as relentlessly as a compass points to the north. I turned to Martin. I said, "You can't let her take the blame."

He looked back at me. His cornflower eyes seemed to be hiding nothing.

"But I didn't do it, Peter."

That probably wasn't a lie. By now he had probably made himself believe it. Martin was capable of that. Martin could kill Sally and lock the memory away in the deepest recess of his mind. Martin only believed what he wanted to believe.

I said, "I'll have to call a doctor now. A doctor will call the police. Do you want them to arrest Marietta?"

He dropped his gaze from mine as if he realized that their blue candour was not working its usual charm. "But I didn't kill Sally. I didn't kill Jake."

Marietta said, soothingly, like a mother, "It's all right, Martin. It'll be all right."

In anger and despair, I said, "You're not to do this, Marietta. I won't let you."

She lifted her green gaze to me. It was as if I were a stranger on the street, stopping her and saying, "Excuse me, madam, but I won't let you breathe." There was an exalted expression to her face, a strange kind of excitement. I realized suddenly that she was enjoying this insane opportunity for sacrifice. Had the martyrs enjoyed their martyrdom that way, I wondered? Thrilling to the flash of the infidel's knife and the touch of the flaming brand to the faggot? The mystery of her was different now—terrible, almost unclean.

178

Iris said, "The lawyer Jake knew in Taxco, he'll send Jake's report to the police, won't he?"

"Yes," I said.

"And it'll all come out about Sally—that she was murdered?"

"Yes."

Quietly she said, "Perhaps they need never know the truth."

I turned to her. I could hardly believe she'd said that. I was too confused to see how anyone could find a way out—however unlikely.

Iris was steady. The idea, whatever it was, had brought her assurance. She said, "We can say Jake killed Sally. We were Sally's friends. We found out about it. We called his bluff. He knew the game was up. He committed suicide."

Martin and Marietta were out of the picture now. It was only Iris and I. I felt a twinge of hope. Iris's way, it would be playing Jake's game back at him.

I said, "It might work."

"You think so?"

Even now Martin was winning, of course. We were all certain he had killed Sally and Jake, but none of us had even considered exposing him to the police. We had moved that far under the Haven spell.

I said, "We'd have to persuade the Taxco police that his report of Sally's death was a lie, something to put the blame on us."

"I know." Some of the light faded from her face. She was thinking, as I was, of the detail, realizing how risky such a plan would be. "There's Sally's letter too. Written on her typewriter. Accusing Martin, Marietta, me."

"Yes."

"Where is it? Did he sent it to the lawyer?"

"No. He said he didn't."

"Then . . ."

Iris glanced around the room. So did I. I saw Jake's gaberdine jacket, where he had flung it, on a chair. I went to it. I felt in the breast pocket. There was a bunch of papers. I pulled them out.

A steamship ticket folder, a letter stamped for mailing, a folded sheet of paper, and an envelope containing prints and negatives.

I unfolded the paper. I saw typewritten words. They began:

"Dear Mr. Johnson,—I've tried to call you. But . . ."

Relief shivered through me. There it was, exactly as Jake had read it out loud to us, Sally's jerky, neurotic cry of danger to her lawyer.

I said, "It's here, Iris."

She hurried to me. She read it over my elbow. "Destroy it."

With Jake dead, there was no one to tell about the overturned vase, the slipper, the broken balustrade. This was the only evidence. I went to the bathroom. I held the half-finished letter over the toilet. I set a match to it. I watched it curl up toward my fingers. I dropped it, black and flaky, into the water. The photographs and the negatives were Jake's two pictures of Sally's living-room. I burned them too and flushed the hopper.

Somehow I felt as if I was killing Sally a second time. This was all that was left of her. Now there was no voice to accuse from the grave.

I still held the other papers in my hand. I went back into the bedroom. Marietta and Martin were together by the window. They weren't even watching. Iris came to me.

I looked at the steamship folder. I pulled the inside paper out. It was a ticket. A single ticket on an Argentine boat sailing the next evening for Buenos Aires.

"The Argentine freighter," breathed Iris. "We saw it in the harbour."

And I realized then that Jake had been a small-time crook after all. He'd been bluffing us when he'd said he was going to stay on. He hadn't had the guts to go on with his game, gradually milking the whole fortune out of Martin. He had been afraid of the situation—and us. He had planned a quick get-away after the first payment. That's why he had brought us to Veracruz—to be near his port of escape.

The killing of him seemed even more futile now. To-morrow, without our lifting a little finger, he would have been gone.

The whole episode would have been over for fifty thousand of Sally's two million dollars.

Just fifty thousand dollars. Money.

I looked at the letter then. It was stamped, but the flap was not stuck down. It was addressed to a Señor Gomez in Taxco. I took the letter out. It was typed in Spanish. I studied it with my threadbare knowledge of the language and suddenly, with a quiver of excitement, I understood it.

It said that Jake was leaving for Buenos Aires. It said that he had left the report for the police with Señor Gomez only for his own protection. Once he was on the boat he no longer needed the protection. He was going to mail this from the boat, he said. When Señor Gomez received it, he was to destroy the report immediately and forget all about it. It was signed by Jake in pen.

It was the natural step for him to have taken, of course. Once he was safe with his fifty thousand dollars, he wouldn't want a murder investigation to flare up around Sally. Not for our sakes. He didn't give a damn for us. But for his own sake. He had been hopelessly tangled in the affair himself. There would be an inevitable kick-back on him.

Even so, as I gazed at those flowing Spanish sentences, this seemed like a preposterously charitable gesture of Fate.

Iris had been reading it too. "Peter, is it . . . ?"

"Yes. When Mr. Gomez gets this, he destroys the report."

"Then we mail it." Iris's face was shining. "And no one will ever know about Sally?"

"No one will ever know about Sally."

There was something to work with now. I felt steady, almost calm. I turned and looked down at the heavy, inert body on the floor. Jake had been poisoned. I knew that. But, to a lay eye, there was nothing about his appearance that glaringly suggested poison. He might almost have died from a heart attack. Big men notoriously had a tendency toward heart trouble. I thought of the carnival. For five days Veracruz had tossed the plodding caution of everyday to the winds. Life was keyed up to accept the extraordinary as the ordinary. Even the policemen, directing the traffic, had been wound in streamers, laughing, joking, part of the annual madness.

A Mexican doctor, coming late at night, through the carnival streets, to attend an American tourist who had died of a heart attack.

Iris said softly. "You're going to mail it, Peter?"

"I'm going to mail it. I'm going down to the lobby right now. I'll mail it and ask the night clerk for an English-speaking doctor."

"A doctor? And . . ."

I turned to her. "I'll tell him my friend had a heart attack. That he'd had them before."

Her lips were pale. "You think . . . ?"

"It might work. Of course, if he's suspicious, if he wants an autopsy, it'll be hopeless."

"And if he does want an autopsy?"

"My friend had financial difficulties. He was morose, neurotic. I'd brought him to the carnival to try to snap him out of it."

She whispered, "And he committed suicide."

"And he committed suicide."

"Peter."

"It's the only way."

"Yes," she said. "It's the only way."

We were doing what I'd always known we would do, fixing things for the Havens.

I looked at Martin and Marietta, standing together at the window. I said, "Get them out of here, Iris. Clear the lipstick-stained butts away, anything that points to people except Jake being here. Then all three of you go to your room. Don't let them talk to anyone. You're out of it now. I'm on my own."

She said impulsively, "Don't you think I'd better come with you?"

In the past, when we'd been in love, she had always insisted on taking her share of any unpleasant responsibility. This unconscious throw-back, coming at this of all times, gave me a pang.

I patted her arm. "No, baby. This is on me."

She smiled fleetingly. "All right."

I went down the stairs into the bare, hushed lobby. The music from the Zocalo was stronger down here. There was a distant explosion followed by faint, high laughter. They were still setting off firecrackers.

There was a mailbox at the foot of the stairs. I stuck the envelope and mailed Jake's letter. The night clerk was dozing behind the desk. I woke him. He spoke English. I told him that my friend had had a heart attack and that I must have an English-speaking doctor at once. An exile from the carnival, he embraced this substitute excitement. He called two numbers and got no reply. He shrugged with dramatic concern.

"In the carnival ees difficult. Even the doctors, they dance."

"I know."

His mouth drooped meaningly at the corners. "I could perhaps obtain Dr. Heller?"

"Dr. Heller? Anything wrong with him?"

He shrugged again. "No ees Mexican. Is from Europe some place. Since many years, he is here and there and . . ."

"Get Dr. Heller," I said.

He called another number. Dr. Heller was available. I waited for him in the lobby. I strolled up and down, smoking. I knew nothing about poisons. For all I knew, the causes of Jake's death might show, screamingly obvious, on the body. Failure to convince this unknown Dr. Heller would mean unqualified disaster. I tried not to think about it. I was afraid thinking would get me rattled.

Within twenty minutes, Dr. Heller came. I joined him at the door. He was old and small in a shabby grey suit. There was about him the generic fugitive quality of a European who has spent many years in foreign countries. He might have been German, Hungarian, almost anything. And I understood immediately the desk clerk's implied contempt. His insecure, almost apologetic manner told of a lifetime spent on the verge of failure, inaugurated perhaps by some scandal in his native land. He was one of those broken, drifting doctors who think of a patient no longer as a patient, but as a potential fee.

The sight of him was reassuring.

I said, "It's good of you to come, Doctor."

As we went up the deserted stairs, I broke the news

that my friend was dead. I said we had come together to Veracruz for the carnival. My friend had had heart trouble. His doctors had advised him not to drink. He had been drinking heavily. To me the story sounded surprisingly plausible and I glanced at Dr. Heller. His dark, faded eyes flicked guiltily away from their study of my ten-dollar Sulka tie. I was almost sure he was calculating in his mind as to whether he dared charge double his normal Mexican fee.

I led him into Jake's room and shut the door. In spite of my growing confidence, it was a moment of excruciating suspense. He dropped his bag and knelt down beside Jake. I watched his old, knob-knuckled hands moving over the body. I started a running patter, the semi-foolish, anxious, plaguing sort of conversation which fitted reasonably with my role of agitated friend and which might also somewhat distract him by taking part of his concentration. I improvised a history of heart trouble and a story of excesses at the carnival. Dr. Heller did not say anything. But, as he went on with his examination and I studied his face, I began to realize that the poison, whatever it was, was not obvious. The death did look enough like a heart attack. Dr. Heller wasn't suspicious. He wasn't even much interested, although he was pretending to be. He was just an old, tired man going through the motions.

At length he unbent creakily.

"Very unfortunate," he said. "Those big men, over-weight, it often goes this way with them."

I could feel relief in me like sweat about to break out on my forehead.

I said, "It's tough, Doctor. You see, he wasn't a close friend. Just an acquaintance who suggested this trip. I don't know what to do, poor guy. I don't know about the law, the . . ."

"He drank a great deal, did he not?"

"A lot, I'm afraid. I tried to stop him."

"And much food, no doubt? And much women?"

"I guess so."

"And he did not take the advice of his doctors?"

"No."

Dr. Heller shrugged. The dark eyes shifted sidelong

from my face. "He has been dead for some time. You didn't find him immediately?"

"No. I came in ahead of him. I went to sleep. I woke up and started wondering whether he'd got in safely. You see, I was always kind of worried. I got out of bed and came here. And I found him."

Dr. Heller nodded. I felt excited, but also slightly guilty that luck should have sent me so minor an antagonist.

I said casually, "It was the heart, of course?"

He straightened his stooped shoulders. He tried to muster some shreds of professional dignity—to give me my money's worth.

"Yes," he proclaimed. "It was the heart."

I wondered how many other wrong diagnoses he had made in the past. I felt less guilty about him then. Perhaps I was the only person whom Dr. Heller had ever genuinely assisted.

I asked, "What do we do, Doctor? I hate to make a fuss for the hotel. Anything like this is bad for them, obviously. I wonder . . . I mean, what is the procedure? There is a death certificate?"

"Yes," said Dr. Heller.

"Which *you* sign?"

"Yes," said Dr. Heller. He paused. "Of course, it is usually advisable to receive from his doctors in Mexico City the entire history of the case before the certificate is signed."

Panic sidled out of some corner of my brain. "But his doctors weren't in Mexico City. He comes from California. I don't even know where. He's only been in Mexico a week or so."

His eyes had moved back to my necktie.

He repeated, "It is usually the case, Mr. Duluth, to obtain the history first."

The slightly emphasized "usually" made me realize he was hinting that this case need not necessarily be usual. I saw then into the pitiful, enforced little shabbiness of his mind. He didn't suspect murder. He wasn't smart enough for that. But he did suspect a rich American tourist who might be willing to pay extra to have a tiresome situation expedited.

He stood fidgeting with the soiled cuffs of his shirt.

I took out my wallet. "You've been awfully kind coming out at this hour. While we're about it, why don't we settle your account. How much do I owe you?"

The faded eyes glinted. "One hundred pesos," he said so quickly that I knew he had taken the daring decision of the doubled fee.

"That seems very little," I said, "I guess I'm used to United States prices. How about this?"

I handed him two hundred-peso bills. His hand clutched for them, but a flicker of exhausted sadness showed in his eyes, as if there was something in him, frail but still alive, which recoiled from venality. The ghost, perhaps, of an earnest, hopeful medical student in a foreign capital many years ago.

He put the money in his pocket. He moved shufflingly to a table and brought out a paper and pen.

"Perhaps in this case, it is more simple for the certificate to be signed now. You are no intimate friend. It is a burden for you to wait, to try to find the doctors, to ruin your holiday, yes?"

"Yes."

"Of course, Mr. Duluth, you try to locate his family, his friends through the *turismo*. Then later you obtain the records and send them to me for my files."

"Of course," I said.

He filled in the death certificate while I stood at his side, giving him the necessary information.

He murmured, "It is necessary to send a formal report to the police, to the American Consulate. And perhaps, too, a letter to the parents if they are alive. Perhaps I can take care of these things for you. But perhaps also it is good for you to stay here a couple more days."

"That's okay with me."

He held the death certificate in his hand. Once again that tired look came in his eyes.

"Perhaps you do not know of an undertaker here in Veracruz?"

"No."

"It so happens that I am familiar with a very reliable concern. I think you will find their work satisfactory—their charges reasonable."

"Anything you say, Doctor." I knew he would obtain

his rake-off from the undertaker too. There had been an interested undertaker in Taxco. There was an interested undertaker here. We had been lucky with undertakers.

Dr. Heller's soft, deflated monologue continued.

"As you say, Mr. Duluth, hotels are most averse to death in their establishment. I am sure they would wish us to—er—remove the corpse as quickly as possible. Unfortunately the undertakers do not have their own ambulances. But I happen to know the ambulance firm. I think you will find their fees . . ."

"Reasonable," I said.

"Yes," said Dr. Heller. "Reasonable."

I thought of Jake being "reasonably" eased into a respectable coffin with this little commission for this little man and that little commission for that little man. It was somehow satisfying that someone who had made such a big noise in life should go out of it like this—to the rattle of small change.

Dr. Heller had stooped to pick up his bag. "We shall perhaps call the ambulance now?"

"Now," I said.

CHAPTER TWENTY-FIVE

Dawn was greying the streets as I walked home from the undertaker. The last of the merrymakers had dispersed. These were the few hours of quiet in carnival. The blustering north wind made the streamers coil and recoil on the sidewalks and sent clouds of confetti dancing like coloured flies through the cold air. Except for minor formalities, the episode of Jake was closed. I could still hardly believe that our huge deception had been so successful.

I was exhausted too. And now that the danger was past, my exhaustion turned into delayed resentment against Martin. I had perjured my soul away to protect him from a murder charge in which he would almost certainly have been found guilty. Now he was safe, relieved from all responsibility. In a few days he would be back in his old life, shaping his childhood memories into yet another novel of wistful, fragile charm, while Iris and Marietta hovered in attendance.

That prospect became suddenly unbearable to me. The danger from Jake had fused us into a dubious alliance, but the danger was gone now. The hopeless tangle of our lives showed itself in all its nakedness. Perhaps I could save Marietta by marrying her. But what of Iris . . . ? I had visions of Iris drifting deeper and deeper into an infatuation which already she knew would bring her nothing. For weeks there had been no talk of that marriage which once had been Martin's passionate goal. I had visions too of Marietta returning to woo her brother like a light-drunk moth beating its wings in a candle flame, Marietta succumbing, Marietta rebelling once again and flying back to me. Life would be unendurable for me with Martin around. Life was impossible for Iris and Marietta too. Martin would never resolve a relationship, begin it or end it. He gave nothing. He waited passively for worship, a worship that destroyed the worshipper. That was his danger.

Sally had ignored the warning signals. Stronger-willed than the others, she had known what she wanted, raped it with the promise of security and fortune, and dragged it to the altar. Jake, in his way, had raped Martin too.

And Jake and Sally were dead.

An old woman with a window frame strapped to her back tottered toward me out of a side street. Life was starting again in Veracruz. Preposterous as it sounds, the fact that Martin had almost certainly murdered two people meant almost nothing to me. He had eaten his way too far into my life for the fate of Sally and Jake to have more than minor significance. It was the thought of what would lie ahead for us that decided me Martin must go.

There were plausible reasons for his own good why he should leave Mexico immediately. It was possible that the lawyer in Taxco might ignore Jake's written request to destroy the report. It was possible too that the death certificate of a doctor like Heller might be discredited. There were a dozen different, if unlikely, accidents which might send the whole edifice of deception toppling. If anything happened, Martin would be trapped. Even he would realize that. And there was no financial difficulty connected with his departure. That very morning, the first payment from Mr. Johnson would be waiting at the bank.

I thought of the Argentine freighter, tied up in the harbour, ready to leave that evening. That was it, of course. Martin, a British subject in Mexico, certainly had a passport. Back at the hotel, I would insist that he leave for Buenos Aires at once.

I was too tired to consider how this might affect Iris and Marietta. The simplicity of the decision brought relief. Let him be gone. Let him wreak all the havoc he wanted to wreak in Argentina.

I reached the hotel. As I passed through the dawn-bleak lobby, where the desk clerk was frankly asleep, I thought instinctively of telling my decision first to Iris. I felt a need for contact with a mind like my mind and the comfort of old acquaintance before I embarked into the foreign land of Haven.

I climbed the stairs to our floor, hoping that Iris would be alone in her room. She was. She had been lying on the bed, but she was still dressed. She looked as exhausted as I felt. There was no strain between us. Because we had suffered the same thing, it was easy being with her.

I said, "It's all right."

She keyed herself up to face disaster. She couldn't quite take this in. I saw that.

"He signed the death certificate?"

"It's all finished. A dingy little doctor with dirty cuffs. All he wanted was a jacked-up fee, a commission from the undertaker, a commission from the ambulance concern."

"He didn't suspect murder?"

"He didn't suspect anything. Don't worry. It's fixed, settled. It's all over."

She dropped down on the bed. The grey early half-light played on her profile.

"It's all over," she repeated.

I sat down next to her. Her weariness and mine seemed the same, like a blanket spread over us both.

She said softly, "I talked to Martin. For a long time."

"You did?"

In a curious voice, she asked, "Peter, do you think he killed them?"

"Yes."

"He swears he didn't. He swears he knew nothing about any poison. It's the same bottle of pills he's had since Taxco. He swears Sally was alive when he left her."

"He might say that."

She turned to me quickly. "I believe him."

Anger spurted. "You! So goddam bedazzled!"

"No." She shook her head. "No, Peter."

"Then . . . ?"

"That isn't Martin. Not to kill people."

"What is Martin?"

She looked down at her hands. "I don't know. But not that."

The anger went. The weariness came back, bleak, with promise of nothing. I saw now what my decision might do to me. Out in the impersonal streets, it had just seemed a way to get rid of Martin. It was different here.

The spell was still on Iris. When I told her that Martin had to go, perhaps she would go too. Perhaps I would lose her for ever. The enforced intimacy which danger had brought had made me forget that already I had faced the prospect of living without her and somehow mastered it. For the last weeks, grim as they had been, at least Iris had been physically there. Slowly, without my realizing it, the need for her had come back.

But the end of my tether was too near. I didn't have the strength to be weak now, to let Martin stay for the useless comfort of having Iris near me.

I said, "I'm going to Martin now. I'm going to tell him he has to leave Mexico."

She glanced up quickly. "Leave Mexico?"

"You can't count on things. Anything might break. It's far too dangerous. He has money, a passport. I'm going to make him take that boat to Buenos Aires to-night."

She didn't say anything.

Dragging the words out, I said, "Will you go with him?"

Her eyes met mine. Her face was stricken.

"Will you go with him, Iris?"

"No," she said.

My hands were on my knees. My knees were trembling. Exhaustion. "Because you're through with him?"

She laughed. "Through with him?"

"Then why?"

"Because I can't." She got up and moved away from me to the window, looking out at the uneventful view of roofs and tree tops. "Because I'm not *that* much of a fool."

"Once you start making a fool of yourself, it's easy to go on."

"No. No, Peter. There comes a time." She turned to me. I saw her silhouetted against the colourless early-morning light.

"I've become such a bitch. I've trampled on everything, my pride, you—everything. I've been worse than Sally, grabbing for him. And I never even got him. It didn't begin like that. It began with me thinking I was sorry for him, thinking I was the strong one. The wise and beautiful Iris Duluth saving the genius from the monster." She paused and added softly, "Who's the monster now?"

She came back to the bed and sat down. She seemed to have brought some of the chilliness of the morning air with her.

"I can't take any more. I lost everything, I know. But I'd rather be like this—with nothing—than have it that way with Martin, going on, on, on. I realized that to-night. I've drunk my fill of Haven."

"It's a bitter brew."

She laughed. "He should start a school. The Haven School for Impairing Your Character and Losing Your Looks in Six Difficult Lessons. With a photograph of me in the prospectus. Iris Duluth Before. Iris Duluth After. Peter, look at me."

"I'm looking," I said. "You're very beautiful."

She shook her head. "No. I'm not beautiful. I'm not anything."

I wanted to take her hand. I wanted everything to be simple again. It couldn't be, of course.

I said, "I'm not much myself."

"You." She was angry. "You've done everything. You took care of that awful thing with Jake. You saved Martin. You saved us all."

"Any guy could have done that."

"No."

"Yes." I said, "What'll you do after Martin's gone?"

"Stay here perhaps. Go back to the States."

"Alone?"

"Who else is there for me to be with?"

I wanted absurdly to say "There's me." But I couldn't. I had other commitments now, commitments which should have made me happy as a carnival reveller because they were going to give me what I had always wanted. I had to tell Iris sooner or later. This was a rough moment to break the news, but we had got far beyond the stage of sparing each other.

I said, "Marietta wants me to marry her."

As I said it, I saw the irony of it. This had begun with Iris leaving me for one Haven. It was ending with my leaving her for another Haven.

I think she was too much out of love with herself to feel the shock. She sat very quietly. "And you said you would? Marry her?"

"Yes."

"When Martin's gone, she'll be rid of him."

"Yes."

She turned to me. "Go to Martin now. Get it over with. Get it done."

CHAPTER TWENTY-SIX

I tapped on Martin's door. It was open. I went in. He was in bed again in the white pyjamas. He was asleep, one arm curled boyishly under his head. The yellow hair gleamed in the strengthening light which was almost sunlight now. I wasn't surprised that he was asleep. I was too used to him. I had been saving his skin. Iris had been agonizing. Martin had been asleep.

I took the arm that circled his face and shook it. He stirred, rolled over, and opened the gentle blue eyes.

"Hello, Peter." He smiled. "Everything work out?"

He spoke as if he had sent me on some frivolous mission. To change a pair of pants, maybe, that had been a size too large for him around the waist.

I said, "The doctor signed the death certificate. He thought it was a heart attack."

He yawned, scratched through his hair with his hand and sat up. "So you were wrong about the poison. I always thought you must be."

"No," I said, "I wasn't wrong."

His eyes clouded. "Then . . . ?"

"There's nothing to worry about. I think we'll get away with it. But we mightn't. Something might happen. It's best for you to leave."

"Leave?"

"Leave Mexico. Right away. There's that Argentine boat. You'll be able to get the money at the bank to-day. You'll be safer in Argentina for a while."

I thought he was going to argue with me, but there was always a point beyond which he was smart enough to abandon his naïveté.

"You really think I should?"

"Yes."

"I didn't kill Jake. I didn't kill Sally. You know that."

"We won't argue about it."

"But I didn't."

"Whether you did or not, the police are going to think so if anything breaks. You don't want to go to jail, do you?"

"Of course not. Besides, I've got the book to finish."

"Yes. Got a passport?"

"Yes."

"Then . . . ?"

"All right, Peter. I'll go." He grinned his quick, friendly grin. "I've always wanted to see Argentina anyway."

"Interesting country, they say. Colourful." This was the moment. I looked at him steadily. "Iris isn't going with you."

I had given up trying to anticipate Martin's reactions. I had no idea what he would say. His face was solemn. The English prefect confronted with a problem that could affect the good name of the school.

"No," he said. "I don't think she should. It wouldn't be good for her. Travelling with a man she's not married to."

"She won't join you later either, Martin. She's had enough."

The blue eyes seemed faintly surprised. Certainly there was no stronger emotion. He said, "She's going back to you?"

"No."

He looked past me toward the sun-splashed window. "I suppose I'm a difficult man for a woman to be around. A writer, you know."

"Yes."

He turned back to me. "I hope she's not too cut up."

"I imagine she'll get over it."

The smile came again, warm, intimate, the schoolboy's smile for his favourite friend. "You've been damn decent about it all."

"Have I?"

"You're not too disgusted with the way I behaved?"

"I guess I'm not."

He looked relieved. "What time's the boat leave, Peter?"

"This evening some time."

He dropped down against the pillow and pulled the bed-clothes up over his slight body.

"Pretty tired. Think I'll get a little more sleep."

"Yes," I said. "Why don't you do that?"

I went back to Iris's room. She was still sitting on the bed.

"He's going," I said.

She looked up. "You told him I wasn't going with him?"

"Yes."

"What did he say?"

"He said he was pretty tired, better get a little more sleep."

She laughed a sudden, small laugh. "That puts me in my place, doesn't it?"

"You can't tell with Martin. Maybe it's a big shock to him."

"It isn't a big shock to him. It's just another burden dropping off."

I went to the bed. I sat down by her and took her hand. "More was lost at Mohatch Field, baby."

Very softly she said, "Where the hell was Mohatch Field, Peter? I never knew."

"I never knew either. But I guess a powerful lot was lost there."

She said, "Did he say again that he hadn't killed Jake and Sally?"

"Yes."

"And you still don't believe him?"

I hadn't really thought about it one way or the other. For me, the problem of the two deaths had become a side issue, almost beneath consideration.

"I don't know, Iris."

"How could he have done it? You have to plan, to be ingenious, to get poison. Martin can't even speak Spanish. Can you imagine him going into a Mexican drugstore and saying, 'Give me some poison, please'?"

"I saw him give the capsule to Jake. There was poison in the capsule. Marietta watched Sally's house. No one went in except Martin."

I remembered then that I had the bottle of sleeping

capsules in my pocket. I had picked them up when I had first gone to break the news of Jake's death to Martin. I pulled it out. There were only five or six tablets left in the vial. I unscrewed the cap and let the tablets roll out on to my palm.

I said, "He undid the capsule, took out the powder, put in the poison, and fixed the capsule together again."

I picked up one of the shiny capsules. I held it vertically and cautiously slid the top half off. The white powder was visible in the bottom half. I took another capsule and did the same thing. But, as I split the capsule, my hand suddenly shook. The white powder was there inside. It looked exactly like the other white powder in the first capsule. But there was a terrific difference.

Trailing up to me from its interior came the distinct odour of bitter almonds.

I stared at Iris. "Prussic acid. Cyanide."

Unsteadily, I fitted the capsule together again. I examined all the others. Three of them were normal. The fourth and last gave out that same, sweet, deadly scent.

A truth came to me then so staggering that it took some seconds for me to grasp its implications.

I said, "It wasn't just the capsule Martin gave Jake. There were two more of them here in the bottle."

Iris was watching me.

"They all look the same," I said. "No one could possibly tell by looking which were poisoned and which weren't. And all three of them were in Martin's bottle. If he'd wanted to murder Jake, he'd have had a special capsule prepared on the side. He didn't. He just rolled one out of the bottle. And there were two more. . . ."

She whispered, "Then Martin *didn't* murder Jake."

"How could he have known which were poisoned and which not? And why the hell would he have had two more of them in his own bottle of sleeping pills, the bottle which no one else ever used?"

I said it then. "Don't you see? Jake's dying was a sheer accident. Those poisoned capsules were put in there for Martin. Martin's the one who was meant to be murdered."

It was hard when I was so tired and spent to have the whole pattern change again. I had grown to accept Martin's guilt. I had shaped everything around that fact.

Martin the destroyer who was to be sent away. Now where were we? Where did we go from here?

Iris's eyes were fixed on my face. I saw my own weary confusion mirrored there.

"Then who, Peter? Jake?"

"Jake? Jake kill Martin when it was only through Martin that he could get his money? Jake let himself be killed in a trap he set for someone else? No, not Jake."

She said, "Do you think I would want to kill Martin?"

"No."

"Then there's only one person, Peter."

She took my hand. She said, "It's better for you to know now, Peter. I tried to tell you earlier, but I couldn't —not when you said you were going to marry her."

I felt a cold tingle up my spine. "Tell me what, Iris?"

"When Martin told me he hadn't killed Sally."

"What do you mean?"

"He told me why he'd let Jake blackmail him, why he'd put up with all this horror. He hadn't been the way we thought he was—just thinking of himself. He had a reason."

She looked away from me. Very softly, she said, "He let Jake blackmail him. And now he's ready to take the blame for both deaths and go off to Argentina. You see, he stands by her too. He's just as tied to her as she is to him."

"You don't——"

"Yes. From the beginning he's been certain that Marietta killed Sally."

The cold seemed to be spreading all through me.

"Because Sally was alive when he left her," said Iris. "And he saw Marietta waiting around outside the house. She could have gone back, you know." She turned to look at me then, and her face was drawn with compassion for me. "I'm sorry, Peter. But, if she killed Sally, then she tried to kill Martin too."

With tormenting clearness, I thought of Marietta fighting against her obsession for Martin, knowing that she would be chained to him as long as he lived, seeing her one chance for happiness with me. Marietta, hating, loving, driven by furies, sneaking the poisoned capsules into Martin's bottle so that Martin would die and she would have her release.

As always, the thought of Marietta brought with it a violent physical reaction. My blood felt like water. Everything in me rebelled against that explanation.

"No," I said passionately. "No. Not Marietta."

Iris's hand was on my arm. There had been that crazy whirligig in time. She was comforting *me* now.

"There's no one else, Peter."

It was the extremity of my want that brought the sudden flash of insight. Like a prayer answered, the realization came that there had been someone else. With an inevitability that was almost uncanny, I saw the real solution, the only solution which brought in every detail and made a uniform design. It wasn't Marietta. The realization seemed to sing in me. It wasn't Marietta.

My voice sounding strangely unfamiliar, I said, "Martin got that bottle of sleeping pills from Sally. I remember. He told me back in Taxco. He had come up to see her from Acapulco. He hadn't expected to spend the night. He hadn't brought his own. And Sally gave him the bottle. She said he'd left it there. The bottle came from Sally."

"Sally?"

"Why did Sally change her mind suddenly? Why did she call you and me and Martin telling us to come to her house at certain definite times? The night before, she had been with me. She had been implacable, eaten up with spite. She had sworn she would never give a divorce, that she would make you all squirm if it was the last thing she did. Why, overnight, did she become sweetness and light?"

A look of half-comprehension had come into Iris's face.

I went on. "Martin said she was pleasant and reasonable with him, told him she would give the divorce. He said she was alive when he left. Why couldn't he have been telling the truth? Martin said she particularly asked him to give her back the gold ring. Why? And why, if no one struggled with her, was the vase overturned, the slipper in the middle of the room? And why did she choose that of all crazy times, after she had made up with Martin, to begin the letter to Mr. Johnson saying she was afraid, that Martin was going to kill her?"

"Peter, you don't think . . . ?"

"When Martin left, Sally gave him the bottle of sleeping pills. And when you arrived, at the exact time she had specified, you found Martin's ring lying on the balcony. Sally must have thrown it there. She was the only person Why did she throw it there?"

Now that I knew, the whole saga seemed as relentless as a steamroller lumbering forward.

"Sally loved Martin—if you call it love. She told me he was the only man in the world she wanted. She was telling the truth. She loved him, and she hated him when she knew she couldn't have him any longer. She hated Martin. She hated you for stealing him. She had always hated Marietta for being closer to him than she could ever be. It was a plan, don't you see, a ruthless, worked-out plan, the sort of plan that could only have come from bitter, vicious malice. From Sally."

I said, "She knew she'd lost Martin for ever. Sally was smart. We've always said that. Sally was smart. She knew things. Once he'd left her with you, she knew she'd lost him and would never get him back. She was going to make you all pay. She said that over and over. *Pay*. She used all her weapons, the bracelet, everything. She went to Acapulco, threatened, and couldn't make a dent. Martin was unthreatenable. He was through with her, and once he's through a person doesn't exist. That's when she must have realized there was only one way to make Martin suffer. And by then her spite must have grown so deep into her that nothing else mattered. Life wasn't worth living if she couldn't get what she wanted, if she had to play the role of the poor little abandoned wife. So she started to make her plan. See, Iris?"

"I think so."

"She hired Jake. That was the first thing. A private detective to protect her. It was an essential part of the plan. She gave Jake the bracelet and the pawn ticket, the evidence against Martin and Marietta for the original theft. She told Jake the whole story of Martin leaving her and dressed it up with fears that he, or one of you, wanted to murder her. Jake was told he'd been hired to protect her from murder. She built him into the perfect witness for the prosecution, when the prosecution should need a witness.

"After that, she came to Mexico City. She couldn't resist going to Marietta and making her 'pay' a bit, because Marietta isn't like Martin. Marietta is vulnerable—through Martin. But Sally's main object was to see me. I had lost my wife to Martin. I was the one person who should have been on her side. She came to me and told me the same story, that one of you was going to murder her. I was meant to be another witness for the prosecution. Only I didn't play ball. She found I was an enemy, not an ally, so she turned on me, too, added me to her list of victims."

As I spoke, Sally was vivid in my mind, the little heavy-haired blonde, the eyes burning with malice, the fragile body exuding danger.

"Everything was set then for the plan. She went home. She called Martin. She called you. She called me. She told us all the same story. Everything would be all right if only we came to see her. Each of us got a definite time. She wanted to be sure that we wouldn't overlap, because the evening was carefully staged as a play with its exits and entrances known in advance. She summoned us all—to a trap."

Iris didn't speak. But I could see the horror, the disgust in her eyes.

I went on. "Marietta showed up. That was the one thing Sally hadn't expected. But it didn't interfere with the programme, because she arrived early. Probably Sally was glad. She hadn't thought of Marietta, but Marietta had fallen into the trap too. And, after Marietta had gone, the real thing began. Martin arrived. Sally was charming, sympathetic, forgiving. She had rehearsed it that way. All she needed from Martin was his presence, his departure, his ring. It ran smoothly. Martin wasn't suspicious. Martin never bothers enough about other people to question their sincerity. He gave her the ring. She gave him the sleeping tablets. He left."

"And after he'd gone," whispered Iris, "before I was due to arrive . . ."

"Exactly. After he'd gone, she staged the scene. The

slipper on the living-room floor. The overturned vase. A struggle. The ring on the balcony. To point that struggle to Martin. And then the letter. It was never meant for Mr. Johnson. She sat down and rattled it off, stopping before the end, trying to make it look as if she had been disturbed in the middle. It was, of course, just something else for the police. A written accusation left behind that Martin or you or Marietta had killed her. Then everything was set for the final act. The demented thing, the only thing she could do to achieve a real revenge on Martin. Maybe she'd saved one cyanide pill from the bottle of tablets. Probably she did, because she could never be sure that the fall would do its work. The timing was perfect. She knew you would arrive any minute. She took the pill out there on the balcony—and she threw herself over the balustrade down to the stream bed."

I added softly, "Maybe you were the one she wanted arrested for the murder. Probably you were, because she'd thought out that other way of dealing with Martin. It looked flawless. You would arrive. You would find her dead. The police would come. There was all the evidence in the world in that house to show she had been murdered. And, even if you had been quick-witted enough to destroy it, Jake would appear. Jake, who had been told she had hired him to protect her from you three; Jake, who had the bracelet and the pawn ticket, the proof of the theft. It must have seemed inevitable to her that she had made you all 'pay' at last.

"There would have been an autopsy. The cyanide, if she took it, would have been the clinching evidence. You would all have been dragged through the courts, and whichever of you was finally convicted, she didn't have to worry that Martin would get off, because she had, actually, killed him already. The cyanide capsules were there in the bottom of his bottle of sleeping pills. She knew he took them almost every day. It was only a question of time. Just luck that he hadn't taken a poisoned one days ago—and died."

Iris shivered. "And it would have happened that way—except for Jake. She didn't figure Jake out right. She thought he was just a stupid hick detective who could be her stooge after she was dead. She didn't realize he was a crook, a smart crook. He came to the house, looking for Marietta. He found the body. He thought one of us had murdered her, of course. But he saw how he could use it for his own advantage, so he ruined her plan, he took it over, he used it for himself."

"Yes."

"It happened that way, Peter. Of course it did."

"It had to. Putting everything together, no one else could have killed Sally, no one else could have killed Jake."

Looking back, it was terrifying to think there could have been that much warped, sadistic spite in one little woman. And yet, it was right. I thought of Sally at the bullfight, bright-eyed while the darts stabbed into the bull. The clue had been there for me from the beginning. The desire to destroy, the desire to be destroyed. Sally had reached the top of her hill all right and found there enough nightmare to satisfy even her.

I thought how her little ghost seemed to have been twittering always close to us through these last terrible weeks. *Really, Peter, it's worth being dead for.* Ever since that night in Taxco, we had, without knowing it, been puppets dancing to her tug of the strings. She'd had her heart's desire, even if it hadn't come in the way she had expected. She'd done it. She'd made us "pay."

The room was quiet. Even Veracruz outside seemed uncharacteristically subdued.

Close to me on the bed, Iris said, "How happy she'd be if she could see us now."

Her voice brought me back. "At least we're not dead."

"No," said Iris. "We're not dead. We fooled her there."

I picked up the bottle which held the capsules. We both looked at it with a sort of horror, as if we were looking at Sally.

Iris's expression changed. A new dread came that seemed to have nothing to do with Sally.

"We'll have to tell Martin."

"I guess so."

Her voice faltered. "And when he knows it wasn't Marietta, he'll know he won't have to take the blame. He won't leave for Argentina."

"Maybe he won't."

Iris seemed to draw herself in, to become smaller. I knew what she was thinking, and pity for her clamped on to my heart like a cold hand.

"Peter, if he doesn't go, it'll all be the same again." She looked up. Her eyes were haunted. "I haven't got the strength to leave him. I'll hang on, hoping, kidding myself, hating myself. It'll go on and on . . ."

She broke off. Her hands clung to my arms fiercely.

"Please, Peter, let him go. Don't tell him about Sally. Let him still think it was Marietta. Let him go."

I hated looking at her. I put my arm around her and drew her close to me. Marietta had cried to me for help, and I had gone to her with all pennants flying. I was going to marry her. Now Iris was crying for help, and all I could do for her was that one small thing. Marietta had me as an anchor. The Havens always found an anchor. It would take months for Iris to find herself again, and there was no one for her—nothing.

If only she had broken down, it would have been easier.

"Don't worry, baby," I said. "Martin will go. I won't tell him anything."

CHAPTER TWENTY-SEVEN

I was back in my own room. I was afraid to stay with Iris. It hurt too much knowing I couldn't comfort her. Sunlight sparkled crisply over the faded carpet. The weather was going to be fine for the last day of the carnival. I had been up all night and felt it. I loosened my tie and dropped into a chair. I took out a cigarette and faced what lay ahead.

The future strangely was Marietta. Sally, Martin, Iris, death, and danger were all in the past. Something new was to begin for me. I tried to recapture those moments, so long ago in memory though not in time, when I had held Marietta in my arms and reacted exultantly to her humble, half-sobbed request to marry her. Somehow the memory was blurred. I found I could not even reconstruct Marietta's face in my mind. At some moment, there in Iris's room, the image had slipped away. I felt obscurely nervous, almost embarrassed.

Some time later the door opened and Marietta came in. The instant I saw her she was alive again to me. She was wearing a green blouse and a white skirt. It is strange what a potent effect clothes have. She had been wearing those things on the night in Taxco when I had found her on Paco's balcony with the garish firework lights bringing her profile in and out of illumination. And suddenly it was the same as it had been the other time. Her beauty intoxicated me. Beneath the shining rook-dark hair, her face was radiant as it had been that night when she had come to me with her sheaf of white stock.

"Peter."

I had risen. She took my arms. Her hands slid up to my shoulders. She kissed me, and I could feel the excitement quivering in her. This was new and strange, wildly removed from the sad tenderness I had left for Iris and which, a few moments before, had seemed so powerful. Strange and unreal as something you dream of happening when you're alone on a dark, rainy night.

I said, "It's okay with the doctor, Marietta. It's all fixed up."

"I know. I know. Martin told me."

She was holding me tightly but with the mention of Martin's name some of the contact between us seemed to go. I felt a strange stirring of anxiety.

"You've seen Martin?"

"Yes."

She moved in my arms so that she was looking up at me. The radiance was there in the green eyes, but something was marring it.

And I knew suddenly what it was. The radiance wasn't for me.

I said, "He's going away."

"I know."

"And Iris isn't going with him."

"No."

Feeling tired and old, I said, "You're going, too. That's what you've come to tell me."

The green eyes were still smiling, clear as the sunlight.

"He needs me."

"Marietta, you're mad. If you go, you'll destroy yourself."

She wasn't listening. I saw now that she wasn't the same person as that crushed, tormented girl who had bared her heart to me with the mercilessness of a Nazi surgeon. That had been Marietta down, out of favour with Martin. This was another Marietta—the Marietta who Martin had summoned into Presence, Marietta up.

I knew then that I had lost her already, if I'd ever had her. This was something beyond argument. And with the clarity of a drowning man, I assessed my love for her. I did love her. In a way that had practically no kinship with my love for Iris. I loved her as, perhaps, a fisherman in a folk legend loved a mermaid, with a love that was doomed never to reach an earthy fulfilment with breakfast cups and morning newspapers.

"Now he has the thing he did to Sally to remember, he needs me. He's always going to need me."

The mermaid image was still there. Her hair, brushing my cheek, was like seaweed. Part of me longed for her and felt a desire to shout out that Martin had not killed Sally, to break through the excuse she had manufactured to justify this ultimate yielding to her obsession.

But I didn't speak. Perhaps that was part of my love too. Perhaps its whole existence was based on the fact that I had known from the beginning it could never reach attainment.

A sardonic twinge of humour mocked me. I had not told the truth about the deaths to save Iris from Martin. As a result I had lost Marietta. But it wasn't really as tidy as that. Marietta would have gone anyway. I saw it now. She had always been tied to Martin as irrevocably as the mermaid is tied to the sea.

She said, "I love you, Peter."

"Do you?"

"Yes, yes." Her face was without sunlight, forlorn. "Yes, Peter."

I looked at her, almost impersonal now, and feeling a pity for her that was stronger than my pity for Iris—or for myself.

"You can't help it, Marietta?"

She shook her head.

"It's gone that far?"

She buried her face against my shoulder. "Don't, Peter. Don't talk about it. Don't talk. Kiss me."

Her lips stumbled to mine. They clung. They were cool and wet as if with ocean spray. Even then, while she kissed me, she had gone from me.

"Remember me, Peter."

"I'll remember you, Marietta."

She slipped out of my arms. In a moment she was gone.

I stood still, the morning sunlight striking warm on my face. I felt as if somewhere in me was a wound. But I felt oddly tranquil too. Did the fisherman feel that way when there was a flash of silver scales and the shore was suddenly empty?

I went to Iris's room. My wife was combing her hair at the mirror. The domestic triviality of the act brought a queer constriction to my throat. She turned, the comb in her hand, shaking back her hair.

"Marietta's going with Martin, Iris."

"No."

"Yes."

She moved toward me. "And you?"

"Me?" I shrugged.

She said, "It feels bad, doesn't it?"

"I don't know."

She was trying to be bright and casual. She was terrified of having me think she would make demands on me now. I knew that.

She said, "And what are you going to do?"

"Iris."

I put my hands on her arms. She was trembling.

"Don't, Peter. You don't have to. Please, you don't have to think of me."

"It's happened before," I said. "People going back."

My fingers knew her skin so well. There was nothing strange. It was like touching myself.

"You can go back a long way. New York, for example. Is New York too far for you? Together?"

She was still trembling, but her face was alight.

"No, Peter. I don't think so. I don't think it's too far . . ."